The Weekend Girlfriend

Emily Walters

The Weekend Girlfriend

Published by Emily Walters

Copyright © 2019 by Emily Walters

ISBN 978-1-09974-913-1

First printing, 2019

www.EmilyWaltersBooks.com

PRINTED IN THE UNITED STATES OF AMERICA

Dedication

I want to dedicate this book to my beloved husband, who makes every day in my life worthwhile. Thank you for believing in me when nobody else does, giving me encouragement when I need it the most, and loving me simply for being myself.

Table of Contents

Chapter 1

"Oooh, that man infuriates me! I don't know why I take his abuse!"

I slammed down my phone and put my head in my hands, feeling the all too familiar pounding of my head beginning to take form.

"Because without this job you wouldn't be able to pay your half of the rent," my best friend, Gretchen Yardley, remarked from across the desk. "And I would have to throw you out."

"You wouldn't dare," I laughed, flicking my pen at her. "Who would make sure you always had booze when you need it then?" Gretchen stuck out her tongue and turned back toward the computer screen, leaving me to brood in silence. It was the middle of the afternoon in sunny Texas, the temperatures rising above ninety degrees and forcing the air conditioner to work overtime to cool the office building. The same could be said of my temper right now, as it was boiling hot just like the weather and directed strictly to the man who signed the paychecks.

For the last three years Gretchen and I had worked for Kyle Thornton, one of the best private attorneys in Texas. He didn't take on cases that he couldn't win and that winning didn't come cheap for those clients either. You didn't use him to get out of a DUI, more like to get out of a murder rap. Most people couldn't afford him, yet his caseload was always full, hence the need for two paralegals (Gretchen and me). It wasn't his work ethic, however, that had me wishing for a bottle of aspirin.

He had called, informing me that he had double-booked himself for this evening with two women and wanted me to cancel one of the dates. "I don't care which one you pick," he had said nonchalantly as if I was picking out a tie. "Just let me know who it was. Try to let her down gently, will you? I might end up needing that cancelled date in the future."

It was harsh, though I doubted he lost any sleep at night over it. And he was telling the truth too. Not only was he the best attorney, he was also one of the hottest bachelors on the circuit. I had to admit that at least, with his dark blond hair and piercing blue eyes, his face chiseled to perfection. Women flushed at the sight of his full lips, the sharp cheekbones and full jaw as well as the way he filled out a tailored suit. Sighing, I forced my thoughts away from my hot-looking boss and looked at the names in front of me, two women that I had no idea who they were.

"Why does he put me in these situations?" I grumbled, pushing the names aside. "I am neither his personal assistant nor his matchmaker." I was a paralegal and should be treated as one!

"Kyle had to fire his assistant, remember?" Gretchen cheerfully replied, her fingers flying over the keyboard. "He slept with her and then, well, you know. She thought she was in love, poor thing. I don't know why the man doesn't hire the male gender. He would save so many broken hearts."

"Well, she was stupid enough if she thought that he was going to treat her any differently than the last. I pity the woman who finally settles him down," I said, thinking about the two names. "Geez, I guess he will go with Rachel tonight. Poor Michelle will have to wallow in self-pity until next time."

Reaching for the phone, I pressed the speed dial for Kyle's preferred florist. I would order the poor woman the usual Kyle floral apology arrangement and perhaps a box of chocolates to smooth things over. Kyle could afford it. I just hoped the woman didn't show up to the office. I could only deal with so much.

***

Hours later, I tucked my feet under me and pulled the fleece blanket tighter around my body as I turned the last page in my sappy romance novel, smiling as always that the guy gave up everything to get his girl. Gretchen was out again with her current boyfriend, Mac. Mac was a gym fanatic much like Gretchen. They met in spin class, where everyone looks like they have been hosed down after it's over. It was so not the place to pick up guys, especially for me. The only thing I had ever met in a gym class was pain and sweat. While I looked like a holy wreck after one session, Gretchen still looked like she had stepped off the cover of a fitness magazine. Gretchen was a true beauty, built like a supermodel with a head full of curly blond locks and baby blue eyes. While Gretchen was gorgeous, Mac was the far end of that spectrum, a tattoo artist with bulging biceps and shaved head.

"He's fun to be around," Gretchen had shrugged when she had told me about him. "And I can't get over those arms. I mean, he could really pick up a car or something." That was Gretchen, looking for someone who could bodily manipulate a steel pipe with his bare hands.

I was the complete opposite of my friend. My selection of men, what little there was, was based solely on availability. After all, I couldn't afford to be too picky. Unlike Gretchen, I was more of an average height, with a few extra pounds lingering, light brown hair and green eyes. I also didn't have an ounce of gracefulness in my body. Actually, I avoided all activities that required some gracefulness. My last date had decided that ice skating would be fun to try, resulting in a long, awkward night in the ER and my wrist in a cast. Needless to say, that had been our last date.

Sighing, I shifted my weight to burrow down more comfortably as I reached for the next book in line, my only date for the night. At least there would be no qualms when I went to bed, alone.

A sudden banging at the front door caused me to jump with a start, nearly falling off the couch in the process. Looking at the clock, I frowned at the time. It was well after eleven, not the social call time for the few that knew where we lived. Our second-story apartment threw out the possibility of a random visitor and most of our neighbors were up in age, way past their bedtimes. Still, I doubted that it was a burglar. Didn't burglars look for easy targets? Why would one choose the last apartment on the second story anyway?

The knocking sounded again, a little gentler this time and I bit my lip as I looked at the door. A burglar didn't knock, right? Whoever it was, I wasn't going to go to the door empty-handed. Grabbing the first object my hand came to, I snorted with laughter as I looked at what was to be my saving grace, a hardback book. What was I going to do, read them to death?

Sighing, I crossed the living room and opened the door a crack, hoping that the chain lock would give me enough time to beat whoever it was to death with a good mystery. The visitor on the other side of the door surprised me though, the book falling to the floor with a loud thud unheeded as I recognized my visitor.

Chapter 2

He was in his dark suit and baby blue shirt, perfectly matching the blue of his eyes. I could see the outline of his broad shoulders, the way his coat opened to show his amazingly fit body underneath. Holy hotness. His face however was a mask of anger, his eyes narrowing as he saw me in the crack of the door.

"Dammit, Jessica open the door," he growled, his arm resting on the doorframe. "I need to talk to you, now."

Stunned, I shut the door momentarily to take off the extra lock, wondering what would happen if I chose not to open it. He sounded super pissed.

Against my better judgment, I opened it anyway, staring at the red face of my boss with trepidation. Yep, this wasn't a social call. "Can I help you, Mr. Thornton?" I didn't even know that he knew where we lived and he had never let on that he did actually know that information.

"You've screwed me, you know that?" he all but roared as he pushed past me to move inside the foyer/living room. "I mean royally this time."

Shocked at his outburst, I quickly shut the door and leaned against it, wondering if I should go ahead and arm myself. I hadn't ever seen him this angry before, not even when I accidentally spilled coffee all over his court notes on the day of an important case. He still clenched his papers tightly anytime I had coffee in my hand and frankly, I couldn't blame him.

"I'm sorry but I have no idea what you are talking about."

Kyle turned toward me and I went still, crossing my arms over my chest to ward off his stare. *Oh great,* I thought, my face flaming in embarrassment. He had caught me without a bra on. To others, it was no big deal but I was super self-conscious about my body and my chest was one place I didn't routinely flaunt for any reason. The only time I went without a bra in mixed company was well, in the dark right before I slept with someone. That particular instance hadn't happened in a long time; a really long time. How freaking embarrassing.

Kyle didn't even seem to notice my bra-free chest nor my embarrassment as he started pacing about the living room, his jaw clenched. I tried in vain not to watch him as he paced, my eyes straying to his oh so sinful body encased in what had to be a new suit since I hadn't taken that particular one to the dry cleaners yet. Since he had slept with his last personal assistant, Gretchen and I had been forced to pick up her slack, including taking his clothes to the cleaners and keeping up with his calendar, until he found time to hire a new one.

He also worked out religiously, his jacket tight across those broad shoulders, the muscles of his biceps outlined as he shoved his hand in his hair. Even though the anger was radiating off him toward me, I was surprised to feel the faint stirrings of desire in my stomach. In the three years I had worked for him, we had never been alone in such a small space. Boy oh boy, he looked too delicious in those pants.

"Do you know who showed up at the restaurant tonight?" he finally asked.

I took my eyes off of his rear end reluctantly to find him staring at me from across the room. Really? Could he not remember the name of the woman he had just had dinner with? Had he really barged into my private space to ask me that? "Am I supposed to know this?"

Kyle threw up his hands in the air, muttering something akin to a curse as he glared at me. "Well, it wasn't Rachel! Of course I didn't know that until I called her by the wrong name. Three damn times."

I felt my cheeks begin to burn as I thought of how I had been on the phone sending the flowers at the same time that a client had walked into the office, demanding attention. I had been so distracted that I had given the florist the first name on the list, which just happened to be... "Oh dear," I muttered, forgetting all about my braless girls and his tight rear end.

"More like dammit," Kyle added harshly. "I have never been so embarrassed in my life. Do you know we were at Mario's when she threw the champagne in my face? Expensive champagne at that. Do you know how many prominent people were there tonight?"

"I'm really sorry," I started quietly, embarrassed. "I didn't mean to do it on purpose." Mario's was a very expensive restaurant uptown, one that people like me could not even afford to sit at and drink tea. Mario's wasn't a restaurant that gave you anything for free. All of the more prominent people in town dined there frequently, so frequently that their reservations were booked well into the next ten years. Kyle was one of those patrons. No wonder he was so mad.

"Well, I can't be so sure of that," Kyle snapped. "I don't know if you did it on purpose to embarrass me somehow. Hell, you could be out to ruin me."

My embarrassment turned to anger as his words sank in. He really thought I was out to get him? For three years I had faithfully taken care of him, supporting him in his profession. When he had lost assistant after assistant, I was the one who had taken care of his love life, sending flowers to heartbroken women and dealing with the ever present phone calls that followed. Blondes, brunettes, and redheads had cried at my desk, reminding me more of forlorn little girls than the successful women they were, all because of him. I had comforted them, assured them, and hell, even lied to their faces on numerous occasions just to keep them from bothering him. There were times I had felt like a therapist instead of a paralegal. How dare he accuse me of purposely trying to ruin his love life! He did that fine on his own. This was the final straw; I didn't have to deal with this mess anymore.

"That's it," I snapped back, throwing my hands up in the air this time. Kyle stopped his pacing and just stared at me, as if I had grown another head. "I am tired of playing to your love life. I am tired of being the one that has to comfort the next Jane, Paula, or Eve when you double-book your dates."

Kyle started to interject, but I waved him off, my blood boiling. I was on a roll and right now, he could call me butter. "I have a degree; I have talents that require a professional working environment. No wonder you can't keep an assistant. No one should have to deal with this nonsense." I then looked him square in the eye, my mind racing to the last possible words I thought I would ever say. "I quit."

"Now wait a minute," Kyle said, a surprised expression coming across his face. "You don't have to quit, Jess. Perhaps I overstepped..."

"You have overstepped for the last time," I replied angrily, crossing the apartment to open the door with such force it banged off the wall behind it. "And only my friends call me Jess. You, sir, are not one of them." I watched him rub a hand over his face and through my anger a tiny bit of doubt started to flame as he walked to the door, looking a bit dejected. What was I doing? I needed my freaking job. How would I pay my bills? No doubt he would give me the worst recommendation possible now. Holy hell, I had burned this bridge.

"You have to give me one month's notice," he finally said, pausing at the open door to look at me, his face emotionless. "It's in your contract. I have to have sufficient time to replace you."

I nodded tightly, not trusting my voice and he left, leaving me to contemplate what the hell just happened. Had I really just quit? Dear Lord, what was I going to do?

***

"I can't believe you up and quit," Gretchen replied tightly as we sat at our desks the next morning. "What are you going to do now?"

"I don't know," I said quietly, the computer screen blurring in front of me. Gretchen was pissed because my brash decision had also hurt my best friend. Without my paycheck, there would be no way we could afford that apartment and unless I found some other job quickly, Gretchen and I would have no choice but to move. That thought was very unsettling with me to say the least. I was hurt but it hurt me more to know I was royally screwing with Gretchen's future as well.

Sighing, I sucked up the tears and clicked on the next job search site. Today was a new day and I had to forge on, starting with the résumés. Maybe I could just leave him off as a reference of past work experience and start all over again. Or maybe I could go to one of his past flames and chalk up a friendship. No doubt they would sympathize with me. Besides, I had all of their contact information in my Rolodex anyway.

The door opened to the office and Kyle walked in, looking splendid as usual in a sharp suit and dress shirt, his blue eyes picking up the moss green of the shirt as they settled on me, causing me to squirm under his stare. Surprisingly, he looked as if he had a rough night as well, his customary clean-shaven face showing a hint of stubble, which instead of making him look horrible, made him look delicious. Maybe it was the guilt he was feeling about the way he treated me, but probably more because he made up with what's her name. Either way, I wasn't going to budge, not this time. My résumés were updated and awaiting delivery. My cardboard box was already picked out.

I forced my gaze elsewhere, back to my computer and pretended I hadn't seen him. I would not break down in front of him. I could do this. He was not the only sexy attorney in town. Well, he was the sexiest but I wouldn't be staying for his sex appeal. Crap, what was wrong with my hormones?

"Ms. Harwell, may I see you in my office?" he asked quietly, his shadow coming across my desk.

Not surprised, I looked up, my eyes colliding with his intense gaze. Maybe he had changed his mind about my contract, wanting to fire me now. How soon could one draw unemployment anyway? By my calculations, my cookie dough budget wouldn't get me through the week. Uncertain whether to turn tail and run to the nearest grocery store now, I stood, smoothing my professional-looking tan skirt over my knees before following his retreating form. I had always thought his office was a thing of beauty, the massive oak desk taking up much of the room. His various diplomas and testaments to his achievements in the community were on display behind him, filling up the built-in shelves that matched the desk. His desk was full of papers and law books, a spillover of the work from the day before. Kyle closed his office door behind me and gestured toward one of his leather chairs that flanked the massive desk.

"I want to apologize for my actions last night," he finally said as he perched on the end of his desk next to my chair. "It was highly improper of me to seek you out for my indiscretions. I acted like an ass."

I was inclined to agree, but I stayed silent, knowing that there was an invisible "but" to the apology. That "but" was going to kill me on the spot, make me move back in with my parents. It was going to throw Gretchen out in the street and force her to reside in another, less desirable apartment.

Kyle sighed and looked down at me, causing me to look away at the eye contact. My nerves were on edge, but I resisted tapping my foot. I didn't want him to see I was on edge. I didn't like to be scrutinized, not in this situation, nor did I like being in this office, alone with him. My job was to be preparing his cases with Gretchen, not having an awkward stare-down in his office.

"I'd hate to lose you," he finally admitted, surprising me. "But I respect your decisions. I know I haven't been the easiest employer."

"Thank you, sir," I replied, stealing a look at his face to see if he was laughing at me. Lord, the man was too attractive for his own good, even with the seriousness of his gaze. I found myself longing to run my hand through his dark blond hair and smooth it, to feel the silkiness under my fingertips. I also wanted to touch his jaw, feel the stubble under my fingers. There was nothing sexier than a bit of stubble on a strong jaw. Oh God, this sexual thinking had to stop, especially about him. Where was this thinking coming from anyway? Sure, Gretchen and I had talked about him and his various attributes in the three years, but I hadn't thought this much into it in a long time. Was it because I didn't have to look at him in a professional manner much longer?

"I do need one more favor however."

It was then I noticed the uneasy look on his face, as if he were uncomfortable at the moment. "It's on the personal nature side of things, I'm afraid."

Chapter 3

I was rooted on the spot, my face rapidly becoming a fiery shade of red. Personal nature? What could that mean? What had I been doing for the last three years? Surely one couldn't put scheduling dates on one's résumé!

"I am a bit embarrassed on having to ask you this," Kyle was saying, running a hand through his tousled hair. "But I have asked everyone and have been turned down by all of them."

Now I was thoroughly confused. Surely he didn't mean anything in that category related to his love life. I mean, I had a Rolodex full of women he could call if he needed a "fix." Hell, Gretchen might even take him up on his offer, she was more of his type anyway. I hadn't seen any women like me coming through his revolving door that was his love life.

"I guess your assumptions were right about my love life," he continued, coming to stand before me, a sheepish look on his face. It didn't help that his crotch was at level with my face. Oh Lord, I was going to combust, incinerate in this chair. "Because apparently I have burned quite a few bridges with the women that seemed to know me the best."

"And what does that have to do with me, sir?" I nearly whispered, not trusting my voice. Oh, the suspense was killing me! Did he need a bed partner, a date, a housekeeper?

"I need you to accompany me to my sister's wedding," he finally said, his voice soft. "In North Carolina. They are expecting to meet my new girlfriend."

"Girlfriend? But you don't have one," I blurted out. He hadn't had a steady bed partner since I had started working for him. Didn't one have to stay around at least a month to qualify for a girlfriend? His women tended to only stay around for a week, two at the most if they were lucky or blond.

"I know," Kyle sighed, his shoulders sagging. "I'm sure you know how parents can meddle in your personal life. It was easier to lie." He then looked at me, his face holding a sly smile. "Now I'm truly caught and you owe me."

"How is that?" I squeaked out, a million questions running through my mind. A girlfriend? He wanted me to be his girlfriend? Could I really be hearing him right?

"You ruined my options for a girlfriend when you got those names mixed up," Kyle explained, crossing his fingers over his washboard stomach. "I was planning on proposing the trip to one of the girls last night. Now neither one of them will talk to me."

"Serves you right," I muttered, crossing my arms over my chest. I was finding it hard to drum up sympathy for him. "I feel sorry for you, sir, I really do but there would be no way I could do such a thing. You will have to find someone else."

"I will double your salary for the next month," Kyle interjected, his voice going up a notch. "And write you a glowing recommendation. I'm desperate here."

I hesitated then, thinking of how much the double salary would help out. It could keep me afloat for one, two months. With a little padding in my account, I could take my time finding a job and not worry about having to leave Gretchen or our apartment.

"I'm not one to beg," Kyle continued. "But I will."

The thought of him on his knees in front of me drummed up some dirty thoughts on my part, causing me to flame once more. Geez. "No funny business?" I finally asked, my voice coming out in a squeak. Funny business? What was I, in a 1960s movie? I really should think of my words before they come out of my mouth sometimes!

"Of course not," Kyle answered quickly, clearing his throat. "Strictly in a business sense. Afterward, you are free to go and I will come up with something to tell my family. Considering my luck as of late, that shouldn't be a problem. I just need you to be yourself, as my girlfriend of course."

I could easily think of a million reasons not to do this, my sense of self-worth, my pride, but considering I didn't have a million dollars to fall back on, the choice ultimately wasn't that difficult. "Okay," I finally said. I was going to regret this, I just knew it.

***

"This is craziness, Jess. I mean who asks things like that?"

"Apparently our boss," I replied, taking a sip of my drink. We were meeting at our usual drinking hole, Mitzy's, a bar that was a far cry from the ritzier ones uptown. Actually, it was one of those places where you didn't wear any shoes without a strap on them, lest you might walk out of them due to the sticky floor. The drinks were cheap, the atmosphere an eclectic crowd of blue-collar workers, college students, and random people off the street, and enough free pretzels to go around.

"I just don't know about this," Gretchen was saying, her hands picking at those free pretzels. "What if you have to kiss him, Jess? What if he decides to make a move on you?"

"He won't," I sighed, thinking that if he did, I would find it difficult to turn him down. It had been two, no three years since I had kissed anyone, much less worry about someone putting the moves on me. I wasn't one for a casual fling, though Kyle would definitely be someone who would test my ability to turn him down.

"You never know," Gretchen grinned, stirring her drink idly. "Honey, I wouldn't put it past him. Who knows? You might be just what he needs."

"Shh, here he comes," I said, watching Kyle walk through the door. A note had been left on my desk a day after his proposition, for dinner and a chance to iron out our story before making the trek to his parents' house. I held my breath as I took in his sexy profile, clad in a gray suit and blue tie, the way the bar seemed to fade away as his eyes locked on mine, a hint of a smile showing on his handsome face. He moved like a predator stalking his prey, drawing looks from every woman in the building as he moved through the crowd.

"You're drooling, girlfriend," Gretchen's voice said just above my ear. "He's smoking hot and I hope you take every advantage of this, Jess. I mean you are practically working on being a virgin again."

"K-Kyle," I stumbled over his name as he approached our table.

"Are you ready to go?" he said, checking his expensive watch on his wrist. "We have reservations."

"Go on, have fun," Gretchen smiled, waving us off. "Don't do anything I wouldn't do!"

I pushed off of the stool and straightened my dress, finding my legs a bit wobbly in the process. I had taken some time with my wardrobe, wanting to let him know I could take this seriously. The wrap dress accentuated my curves and the girls, or so the saleswoman had said, paired with my favorite pair of sling-backs in a deep red. Right now I felt like I was walking on stilts, the effects of two vodka and cranberries hitting me hard.

I followed Kyle out of the bar and into the warm evening, the sun just setting behind the buildings in front of me. A sleek, silver Porsche waited at the curb and I felt the first stirrings of nervousness build at what I was about to embark on as Kyle held the door open, letting me slide into the leather interior. I had never ridden in a Porsche before and as Kyle climbed into the driver's seat, the closeness of the interior filled immediately with his expensive cologne. "I like your car," I said, unsure of what to talk to my boss about other than work. "It's small."

"Well, that's the whole point," Kyle chuckled as he expertly shifted the gears. I found something extremely sensual about that movement for some reason. "I don't find myself having issues with parking."

"Oh well, that's good," I said, swallowing as I looked away from his long fingers and the dirty thoughts that seemed to follow.

"Don't be nervous, Jessica," he said softly, looking at me with those gorgeous eyes of his. "We will get along just fine. Just relax."

"I'm fine," I said softly, forcing a smile. "Where are we going to eat?"

Kyle's eyes shifted back to the road as he moved in his seat, his jaw working in the dim light. "I lied when I said we had reservations."

"Oh," I said, a little bummed that I had bought this dress for no reason. Maybe Gretchen wouldn't come home for a while and I could make up a story. I didn't want her to know he had actually stood me up. "Okay, well it's not anything important if you don't want to go out. I can wing it."

"Oh no, I have plans," he interrupted, cutting me off. "But we will be going to my house for dinner."

"You-your house?" I asked, truly intrigued now. I had never been to his house before, only knew his address to be in the nicer neighborhood and a long way from my apartment along the highway.

"Yeah, I couldn't take the chance of rumors," he said, his jaw tightening. "I hope you don't mind."

"No, of course not, I understand," I stumbled through the words. Of course, we weren't to be a real couple and to be seen in public would have rumors running rampant. That was why he picked Mitzy's to meet me. Though it was practical thinking on his part, I couldn't help but feel a twinge of hurt in the process. No woman wanted to be hidden, tucked away from prying eyes and felt to be a secret instead of a prize. Shaking out of it, I forced a smile as he turned the car into a gated community, the houses like something out of magazines. I had no right to be hurt because he didn't want to be seen with me in public. We weren't supposed to be.

Kyle made a few turns and finally pulled into a driveway, guiding the car into a large garage before killing the engine. I opened the door and crawled out as ladylike as I could, noting the BMW and large SUV occupying the rest of the space. Yep, he was definitely successful. No doubt he would get a good laugh if he saw my beat-up Honda.

"This way," Kyle motioned, climbing the stairs to a side door and opening it, the chimes of an alarm system echoing in the dark space. I made my way through the door and into the welcoming air conditioning, finding myself in a dimly lit kitchen. It was massive, lined with stainless steel appliances, granite countertops, and dark cabinetry. A large island sat in the center, the décor looking like something out of a magazine. Kyle set his keys in a bowl on the island and motioned for me to follow him, my heels clicking against the tile floor as he led me through the dining room, which looked rarely used, out to a patio that overlooked a golf course. A table was set up near a covered hot tub, the candles flickering in the warm night. It was intimate, much more than any cozy restaurant would be and I begin to get nervous again, way out of my element.

"I don't cook much," Kyle was saying as he led me over to the table. "So I ordered out. I hope you like steak."

"Steak's fine," I said, taking a seat on the cushioned chair. There was a salad, no doubt from some restaurant I'd never visit, and a glass of cold red wine near each place setting of delicate china. An elegant warming dish in the center of the table was no doubt keeping the steak at just the right temperature.

Kyle sat across from me and took a sip of his wine, his eyes focused on me as I sat there, unsure of really what to think. "You have a lovely house," I finally said, looking around the backyard. "I hope you have really good coverage on your windows, being this close to the course."

"I have excellent coverage," he laughed, the deep sound causing my cheeks to flush. "I hope this isn't making you uncomfortable. I confess someone else set all of this up and apparently thought it was supposed to be romantic."

"I'm sure they were just used to your other dates," I said wryly, taking a big sip of the wine. I didn't usually like red wine and was surprised at the fruitiness as it slid down my throat.

"You are probably right," he grinned, a hint of dimples showing on his face. Oh God, they were downright sinful. "So, what should I know about you?"

"Well, I am an only child," I started, feeling the effects of the wine calming my nerves. "My parents live in Arizona. I like to read, I love cookie dough, and Gretchen is my best friend."

"Any past engagements, criminal records?" he asked, his long fingers drumming against his glass.

"No, no nothing of the sort," I smiled. "I'm a very good law-abiding citizen. What about you? Anything I should know about?"

"A brother and sister, both older than me," he said, frowning. "Overbearing parents who think I'm a screw-up, a black sheep. Do you need some more wine?"

I was stunned by his admission as I held out my glass to him, allowing him to pour me some more with those long fingers of his. "But you are so successful," I blurted out, pulling my glass back. "I mean look at your house, your car, your successful practice. You are one of the best attorneys in Texas. Surely they would be proud to have you as their son."

Kyle looked up at me with a surprised look on his face, a smile hovering on his gorgeous lips that didn't quite reach his eyes. "You think I'm the best?"

"I said one of the best," I shot back, noting how he was turning the conversation away from his parents. Great. I didn't think it was going to be easy to win over the people who knew him best but now that I had some history, it was going to be damn near impossible.

"See? This is why I picked you, Jessica. You can hold your own," he said, his grin becoming wider. "I am glad to see I didn't make a mistake."

"You didn't have much of a choice," I grumbled, wondering if I should be offended or flattered. I was surprised at how easily I was having this type of banter with my boss of all people, someone I hadn't talked to in any other way than work related. It was nice to know that he wasn't as bad as I thought, though those wicked grins were starting to have an effect on me.

"We should eat," he said, draining his wine. "Or I can give you a tour of the house, your choice."

"Tour," I said, my stomach still too nervous to eat. Picking up my glass, I followed him indoors, where he shed his jacket and tie to my surprise, unbuttoning the first couple of buttons on his shirt. I struggled to keep my mouth closed as the small patch of golden skin came into view, the desire to run my fingers over his chest hitting me full force.

Ruffling his hair, he grinned at me, looking much younger than I had originally thought. "Kick off your shoes, make yourself at home, Jessica." I wanted to touch him, but instead I kicked off my heels, feeling my bare feet sink into the plush carpeting as he showed me the living room, a massive TV above the stone fireplace that dominated one wall of the large room. Here I felt marginally better, the furniture was dark but comfortable-looking. I could easily see him lounging on the large sofa, watching his Cowboys play football when he didn't attend the games, since I knew he held season tickets. His house was masculine in nature with the furniture and wall colors, but airy and surprisingly modest given the neighborhood.

Upstairs, he showed me three spare bedrooms and another bathroom before throwing open the master suite doors, his spicy scent drifting out of the room. It was a large bedroom, a king-sized bed taking up much of one wall with dark furniture dotting the others. I tried not to think of him sleeping on it as we walked past, where he had a large bathroom with a whirlpool jetted tub and glassed-in shower. A pair of French doors stood open and I walked out to find a large round chaise lounge on an iron balcony, overlooking the course as well.

27

"Wow, you just have to have the biggest bed in Texas, huh?" I teased, draining my glass. My head was swimming a little, but I felt deliciously warm and more at ease. Liquid courage at its best. "I'm sure the ladies really like it."

"Actually you are the first woman in a long time I've had in this room," he grinned, leaning against the doorframe. "I can't take the chance of stalkers and the like knowing where I live. I usually end up leaving their beds."

"Wham, bam, thank you ma'am," I said with a smile. "Smart."

"I don't know if I consider it that," he laughed, his eyes twinkling. "But you of all people know I like my women."

"I don't think there's many left," I replied, hiccupping. "Maybe Shirley in the doctor's office downstairs. I don't think you have hit on her yet."

"Yeah well, she's fifty," Kyle reminded me. "But I didn't have to do anything. She hit on me, trapped me in the broom closet. I had never felt so dirty from getting hit on by an old lady before."

"Oh my God," I giggled, gripping the railing. "That is too funny."

Kyle had the grace to blush and I felt the warmth spread to my toes, taking in the simple sight of him. "And there's Gretchen," he continued, pushing off the doorframe. "But she's a bit intimidating even for me."

"I think you could take her," I swallowed as he took a step toward me. "She's dating someone right now but that's never stopped her. Oh I didn't mean she's a slut or anything."

Kyle's grin grew wider as he stopped before me, reminding me of how tall he was. I barely reached his shoulders, I realized as I looked up at him. "And there's you."

"Me?" I squeaked out as he reached out, barely touching my cheek with his fingers. "But I'm not... I'm not even your type."

"How do you know what my type is?" he said softly, leaning down until our lips were within inches of each other. I swallowed a retort as his lips covered mine, first with a hesitant kiss then when I moaned, then taking my mouth full-fledged. I felt his lips rub over mine, his tongue barely touch my lips, causing me to gasp and give him ample opportunity to slip it in. He tasted like wine and the barest hint of brandy, a delicious warmth that spread like no wine could as his tongue tangled with mine, stroking, touching.

Taking my hands, I slid them into his hair, pulling him closer to feel him against me. His hands slid around my waist, holding me against him as I felt the hardness of his body against mine, the delicious shock of what made him supremely male rubbing against my stomach.

"Jesus," Kyle whispered against my mouth, rubbing his lips over mine. I trembled as his hands stroked the small of my back, tracing my spine and sending sparks of desire throughout my body. I felt sexy, powerful having this man in my arms, kissing me.

"I want you," he said softly, his hands gripping my hips, pulling me hard against him. My head was spinning wildly as his hands started to dance around my hips, down my arms and across my shoulders. "Let me pleasure you, Jess."

"I haven't given you permission to call me Jess," I gasped as his lips nibbled at my neck. Good lord, this was what all of those other women wanted from him, what they felt with him. No wonder he was so popular. I felt him chuckle against my neck, his lips moving to tug gently at my earlobe, sending a bolt of desire through me.

Then the worst possible thing happened. I pulled away from him, no, shoved him off me and ran to the bathroom, holding my hand over my mouth the entire way.

Chapter 4

"Go away," I moaned resting my head against the toilet bowl. I was beyond caring how disgusting that sounded, having spent the last hour locked in the massive bathroom hugging my boss's toilet. I was humiliated that I had nearly thrown up on him in the first place, much less stuck in his bathroom.

"Come on, Jess," he said, his voice barely audible through the door. "At least come and get this ginger ale. I swear it will settle your stomach."

"This is so beyond embarrassing," I muttered, pushing myself off of the floor on wobbly legs. Truth be told, I did feel much better. Apparently sweet wine and vodka on an empty, nervous stomach were not a good mix; not to mention the extracurricular activities that had me overheated.

Sighing, I washed my mouth out with the mouthwash I had found in the cabinet before unlocking the door. Kyle stood on the other end, holding a soda can and two pills in his hand, a concerned look on his face. "Are you okay?"

"I've been a hell of a lot better," I muttered, leaning against the doorframe.

"Take these and drink this," he said, handing me the drink and pills that would hopefully be my saving grace. "I've got some crackers if you feel like you can eat something."

"Ugh, I don't want to even think about food," I replied, taking the pills with a swallow of the ginger ale. "I'm sorry about your bathroom."

"Don't worry about it," he shrugged, reaching out to touch my cheek. "Come on, let's get you into bed."

I froze, the look on my face must have been priceless for he chuckled, dropping his hand. "No, not like that. You need to rest and I have plenty of spares."

"I need to go home," I said wearily. I had already overstayed my welcome in the bathroom, humiliated myself to no end in front of the man who was my boss, and all I wanted to do was crawl into my own bed and cry.

"No," he said, crossing his arms over his chest and giving me his best don't mess with me stare. "You need to rest and I have an early morning case that I need to work on. I can drop you off on my way in but not before."

"Fine, whatever," I sighed, too tired to argue. "Lead the way."

Kyle smirked as he led me over to his bed, picking up a T-shirt in the process. "Here. I don't wear pajamas but this is a clean shirt. The sheets are clean, I assure you."

"Oh no no, I can't take your bed," I protested, holding up my hands. Taking his toilet was one thing, but sleeping in his bed was a whole other level.

"I insist," Kyle said, handing me the shirt. "Good night, Jess." He then strolled out of the room, giving me a great shot of his rear end in the process.

"Ugh," I repeated, turning back to the bed, my head pounding. I had totally screwed up a chance to sleep with the hottest guy I had come across in my adult life, embarrassed myself by having a heart-to-heart with his toilet, and now was going to sleep in his bed, alone. Life couldn't get much worse.

Sighing, I shed my dress and pulled on his shirt, enveloped immediately by Kyle's spicy scent. The shirt was well worn and comfortable, falling to mid-thigh. I climbed into his bed after some hesitation, finding the sheets were indeed freshly smelling and cool against my bare skin. After cutting off the lamp, I stared into the darkness, the house silent around me. This wasn't how I had envisioned this night at all, though at least I could tell Gretchen I had accomplished getting into Kyle's bed, without him. I thought of his kiss and smiled, knowing that it would have to be at the top of the best kisses ever. Would the next one be just as passionate and exciting or would we drift into the show of a lifetime in front of his family? Had I just missed an opportunity to delve deeper into uncharted territory with him?

***

"I can't believe you upchucked in his bathroom," Gretchen laughed, pressing her lips together as she saw my dark look in her direction. "I swear, Jess, you have the absolute worst luck ever."

"Yeah, well at least you don't have to spend an entire weekend pretending to be his girlfriend," I grumbled, turning back to my computer screen. It had been a very quiet ride back to my apartment this morning, Kyle barely making eye contact as he had driven me. I had woken up in a foul mood as well, my dreams filled with him and what might have been. Kyle had been waiting in the kitchen for me, handing me a cup of hot coffee in a travel cup before leading me to the BMW. I tried but miserably failed not to notice how sexy he looked in his charcoal grey power suit, with blue shirt and tie, his jaw freshly shaven. I found myself longing to mess him up, to make him look less formidable and more like the man who had drunk wine and kissed me only a few hours ago.

Now I sat at my desk, glancing at the door every few minutes to see if he was going to appear. Gah, this sucked. How was I going to survive an entire weekend? The last thing I wanted to do was make this awkward between us, especially at work but I would be kidding myself. This entire situation was going to be awkward regardless of what happened.

The door opened and Kyle walked through, his suit jacket slung over his shoulder like he was modeling for the cover of GQ. He could easily do it, but that was beside the point. His hair was standing on end, as if he had run his fingers through it a few times and his tie was loosened, signaling a horrible court day. We had long since learned that if he came back to the office after a court day, then it had not gone well. If he had a successful day, then he cleared his calendar and went out, presumably to find himself some company or get roaring drunk. Either way, he always came back with a smile the next morning.

"My office, now," he grumbled as he passed, never passing a glance in my way. Considering Gretchen was gone for the day, I could safely assume he was talking about me.

Gathering the documents that pertained to today's case, I dragged my feet to his office, where he was sitting behind his desk, his head in his hands. Immediately my mood softened and I felt a twinge of guilt, hoping that our messed-up night hadn't caused any of this stress. Acting on impulse, I set the papers down on the desk and maneuvered behind his chair, my fingers sinking into the softness of his hair.

He stiffened and I hesitated, wondering if I had overstepped myself. It was totally improper for me to be doing such a thing to my boss, yet pretending to be his girlfriend had to be worse at this moment.

Holding my breath, I dragged my fingers up and down his head, receiving a groan in response, a smile stealing across my face. I had been on target with what he needed.

Trailing them down his neck I kneaded the muscles on the back of his neck, then his shoulders, which were unbelievably tight under my touch. "Bad day at the office?" I asked softly as I worked on his shoulders.

"Not at the office," came his muffled reply, his face still buried in his hands. "Court yes. I don't know if I am going to win this one. My client is a dumbass."

"Well, most of yours are. You wouldn't have a job otherwise."

"I guess you are right," Kyle chuckled, lifting his head. "God that feels good, Jess."

"Maybe I should market this," I said wryly, running my hands back up to his tense neck. He felt pretty good himself, the strong muscles bending and shaping under my fingers. I longed to run my hands under his shirt, feel his bare skin under them, and the thought of doing just that sent chills down my spine.

"Maybe I should keep you around just for this," he replied, spinning his chair around to look at me. It was then I saw the dark circles under his eyes, the exhaustion setting in on his handsome face.

"Maybe you need to sleep," I suggested, dropping my hands, the easy bantering gone. It was obvious he needed rest, not someone babying him. His eyes bore into mine as I stood before him, his hands reaching up to grasp my hips, pulling me into the V of his spread legs.

"I tried last night," he said softly, his fingers resting just above my hips. I had dressed conservatively today, with a pair of dress pants and shirt that was modest, even for me. Still, I could feel the heat on my skin as if I were naked before him. "But someone was occupying my bed, someone sleeping on my sheets."

"You told me to," I reminded him gently, bringing up my fingers to brush his jaw, now prickly with a five o'clock shadow. I knew I shouldn't be touching him, but I couldn't help myself, my fingers trembling as I cupped his cheek with my hand. He was made for touching. Kyle's eyes were a steely blue as I brought the other hand up and framed his face, leaning down to brush my lips across his gently, feeling his hands tighten on my hips. "Go home and go to bed," I whispered against his soft lips, leaning back when he tried to deepen the kiss. "Get some sleep. We can't run this joint without you doing what you do in that courtroom. You don't want to put us out on the street, now do you?"

"Come with me," he said raggedly, pulling me back against him. "I can think of other things that could lull me into a good sleep." I could feel his arousal and found myself wanting to give in, find out how good he really was in bed, and move on. However, I knew I would be doing more to myself than just a romp in bed with him. I would be getting involved, way over my head and come out on the wrong end of this deal. Casual sex was what he did, it wasn't me.

"I can't," I finally said, pushing my way out of his embrace and putting some distance between us. "Good night, Mr. Thornton."

Kyle stared at me for one long minute and then let out a breath, turning away from me. "Good night."

Chapter 5

Saturday, glorious Saturday.

I smiled as I woke up to sunshine streaming through my window, stretching out the kinks. After a fitful night of sleep, I was glad to see that I would not have to endure the tension building between Kyle and me for at least two days. Still, I couldn't help but wonder if he had slept well. Ugh, this was rapidly becoming personal and we hadn't even done our big performance. He shouldn't be occupying my thoughts as he was doing on my day off. He was my boss, for God's sake.

Throwing back the covers, I padded to the kitchen barefooted, pouring myself a cup of coffee.

"Jess."

"Oh my God," I squealed as the coffee mug slipped out of my hand, falling into the sink with a loud crash. My hand flew to my chest as I eyed Kyle standing in the living room, his arms crossed over his chest and a small grin on his handsome face. If I thought he looked hot in a suit, he looked scorching dressed down in a blue polo and jeans that clung to his legs in a way that had to be illegal. "What are you doing here?"

"I thought we could spend the day together," he frowned, pulling out his cell. "Didn't you get my email?"

"It's Saturday!" I protested, my hands flying to my hair, which no doubt was all over my head. Luckily I was wearing a pair of sleep shorts and a T-shirt, my usual sleeping attire. "I don't check emails after I leave the office."

"Gretchen let me in on her way out," he said without an apology. "We need to spend some time together, Jess, before next weekend."

"But, but," I started. It was my day to lounge around, do some retail shopping, and gorge myself on Chinese food; not spend time with my boss!

"I've made some plans for us," he continued as if I wasn't even speaking. "A ride around the bay on my boat, some lunch. I won't force you to spend all the time with me, just some of it."

"You aren't forcing me," I grumbled. Like it would be such a hard thing to spend time with him. "Did you say boat ride? You aren't talking like an old fishing boat, right?" I detested any boat without a motor and less than three seats. Another date gone horrible had caused that hatred. One dunking in a murky pond and most people would be inclined to agree.

"Much, much bigger," he winked. "I doubt it will disappoint you in the least."

I went warm as I thought of the night before, the sexual innuendoes that had been happening between us. Was I even safe to go out in the middle of the bay with him? Could I fight him off if he really turned on the charm? Did I really want to? "Alright, give me some time to get ready," I sighed. At least it would be a gorgeous day and I would be on the water, not at work.

"I will be right here," he smirked, his expression smug knowing that he had won.

Damn him. Leaving the shards of my mug in the sink, I stalked back to my room and pulled out a pair of white shorts and a blousy tank top, knowing that it concealed my problem areas but showed off the girls without looking slutty. Well, there were two ways to look at this. Either he really wanted to get to know me or get in my pants. Either way this was going to be an interesting day.

Throwing on the outfit, I ran a brush through my hair and applied the lightest of makeup, choosing a pair of strappy sandals to complete the look. It must have been fate that I had just shaved my legs last night or else he would be waiting a long time. Grabbing my purse and a light jacket, I made it out of there in under ten minutes.

"I don't think I have ever met a woman who could get ready so fast," Kyle remarked as I entered the living room again. "You look good, Jess."

"Thanks," I muttered, still not over the fact he was ruining my perfect Saturday.

Kyle just chuckled as he ushered me out of the door. "I promise to make this a relaxing trip. No work, just a bit of fun." I bit back a smile as I saw the Porsche at the curb, wondering if he had remembered my remarks about this car, or was it just wishful thinking that he had been actually paying attention to me? Sliding into the cool interior, Kyle threw it in drive and we were off.

"Did you sleep well?" I asked as we zoomed toward the bay.

"Not really," he said, sliding a glance over at me. "I spent much of the night planning this and sending you emails you apparently don't read."

I didn't know how to take that he had planned something with me in mind, my nerves still on edge at what I was getting myself into today. "Not everyone is a workaholic," I finally remarked. "Some of us actually enjoy not being at the office."

"Well, I plan to spend my Sunday and Monday there," he replied, shifting gears. "I've got to get this case wrapped before we leave Tuesday. My parents have a hellacious week-long list of things going on."

My mind went back to the real reason we were spending time together and how it would all be up in the span of a week and I would be out of a job. Being his girlfriend was becoming easier by the moment but the added bonus of what I was likely to experience at the hands of a family with serious issues was going to be tough. Truly, I couldn't see why there was such a discord with his parents. Yes, Kyle was a womanizer, but he was an excellent lawyer who took his job very seriously. He also was a great boss for the most part, giving me and Gretchen substantial bonuses around the holidays and four weeks' vacation each year. He irritated me, had me cursing his name a time or two, but truly it had been a very good place to work the last couple of years. I was going to miss it, miss him.

Kyle pulled the car into a parking spot and we climbed out, the view of the bay taking my breath away. Though warm, it was a gorgeous day to be on the bay and as he stopped in front of a pretty good-sized boat, not quite a yacht but definitely not a fishing boat, I found myself smiling. "Okay, you were right, I'm not disappointed."

"It's not much but I like it," he said as he helped me on board. I was quickly shown the small galley complete with kitchenette and bedroom, all decorated much like his house, with a tasteful, out of a magazine feel.

"I didn't even know you had a boat," I remarked as I stood next to him, watching him start up the engine and do all that other boat stuff I didn't understand.

"There's a lot about me that you don't know," he grinned, slipping on his aviator sunglasses. "Have a seat."

Intrigued, I sat down in the chair next to his and we were off, drifting the boat out of the dock and out into the middle of the glassy sheet of water before gunning the engines. He was right of course. There was so much I didn't know about him, and I was finding myself pleasantly surprised at what I was finding out on a daily basis. He was rapidly becoming less like the hard lawyer I knew him as and more like just a regular man, one who was dangerously worming his way into my life.

I closed my eyes against the thought and allowed the sun to seep into my pores, the occasional spray splashing my face. This was the life. I loved being in the sun, preferring the beach any old day. After my duties were done and I had the extra money to keep me afloat for a while, I would be doing just that for at least a week. We cruised for a while before Kyle killed the engines and dropped the anchor, a large smile now on his face, his hair windblown and nothing like the man from yesterday. I looked around and saw that we were the only boat for miles around, smaller dots barely discernible in the distance. It was quiet and warm and I found myself smiling. "This is really nice."

"Absolutely," Kyle replied, reaching into his pocket for his phone. "I'm going to cut this off and then go for a swim. Wanna join me?"

"Yeah right," I laughed, reaching down to remove my shoes. "No bathing suit on this person."

"I didn't ask if you had a suit," he grinned, throwing his phone on the seat. "I asked if you wanted to swim."

"You're joking, right?" I said, eyeing him, looking at his body, then down at mine. Yeah right, he might be able to do that, but I didn't like to be in a bathing suit, much less seeing myself naked. "It's daylight and I do believe skinny dipping is frowned upon when the sun is up."

Kyle's grin got wider as he leaned over me, placing his arms on either side of my shoulders, caging me in. "I didn't say anything about doing it naked, though that is one of the best ideas I think you have ever had."

I shivered at the thought as he touched my nose with his fingers and pulled away, pulling his shirt over his head in the process. Holy hotness, I thought as I watched his tanned skin come into view, his washboard stomach glistening in the sun. His chest was a thing of beauty, his pecs well-formed and biceps flexing under the movement. A light dusting of dark blond hair covered his tanned skin, forming that oh so popular line down his midsection and disappearing into those jeans that were about to be shed.

"Enjoying the view?"

Red faced, I forced my gaze away from him, clearing my throat. Good God, the man was sinful all the way around. "I think you are on your own with your swim."

"I dare you," he answered, forcing me to meet his gaze. "Come on, Jess. When's the last time you lived a little? Did something completely out of your norm?"

"Let's see, accepting your fool plan," I shot back, my mouth going dry as he shucked his jeans. Thank God he was wearing boxers, I might have fainted at the sight otherwise. It was hard enough not to notice the impressive package outlined by the thin material. He was gorgeous and I longed for just a touch, a small one without any complications. He was like chocolate and I was afraid at one touch I wouldn't be able to stop.

"That doesn't count. You are getting something out of that as well," he reminded me, pulling out the ladder and lowering it into the water. "Try again."

I opened my mouth but found myself unable to find anything else that would compare to what he was asking at this time. When had been the last time I had done something daring, something totally out of my norm? Had I ever done that?

Kyle gave me a salute and lowered himself in the water, his head barely visible over the side as I swallowed, weighing my options. Undergarments counted as bathing suits, didn't they? Was I really considering this? I wasn't ashamed of my body, a little disgruntled with it at times, but knew that I was unlike anything he was used to seeing. I had an extra few pounds around the middle, my girls were big and proud, and I found nothing sexy about being in my underwear. Still, I thought as I toyed with my top, this was a chance of a lifetime. This wasn't going to lead to anything in particular, right? After next weekend and a suitable replacement, I wouldn't have to see him again if I didn't want to. Shit, I was really going to do this. Gretchen would be so proud.

Taking a deep breath for courage, I took off my top and shucked my shorts. Thank God I had sensible underwear on, but my bra, well I might as well not have one on. Lacy and see-through, it was going to be near transparent when wet and I could only hope Kyle would be a gentleman and keep his comments to himself and his head above water. Somehow, I knew that was not going to be the case.

Stepping over the side, I lowered myself in the warm water, grateful it was so hot outside. Kyle's eyes never left mine as I attempted to doggy paddle in his direction, finally reaching him without drowning myself.

"See?" he said, his eyes twinkling. "That wasn't so bad, was it?"

"Like pulling teeth," I muttered, pushing my hair out of my eyes.

Kyle held out his hand and I grabbed it, allowing him to pull me to where he was. "There's a sandbar here so you can stand," he explained, guiding me until my feet hit the warm sand.

As I stood, I realized that the majority of him was out of the water, the water playing peekaboo with the waistband of his boxers. That meant my top half was out of the water as well and I flushed dull red as Kyle's eyes strayed to the girls, swallowing hard.

With a gasp I attempted to duck back into the water, but Kyle's arm shot out, pulling me back to my standing position. "Don't."

His expression was tight as his hand moved up my arm and over my shoulder, drifting lower until he cupped my bra-covered breast, his thumb flicking over my already erect nipple. Sensation coiled through me at the contact and I whimpered as he moved to the other, bringing up both hands until they covered my chest adequately. It was heaven, it was hell as he growled low in his throat, stroking the tight peaks until I was sure I was going to combust just from the touch.

"Jesus," he whispered, his fingers dancing along the material before reaching in and pulling both out of their confines. "They are gorgeous."

"Please," I whispered, feeling wanton yet embarrassed at the same time. I wasn't entirely sure if my please was to continue or to stop at this point. We were in the shadows of the boat and unless someone came real close, there was no way we were going to be disturbed for now. It was the most risqué thing I had ever done.

Kyle's eyes darkened as he traced a lazy circle around my nipple, lifting my breast as if testing the weight of it. I moaned when he crossed over the naked nipple and he lowered his head, his teeth grazing the aching bud and nearly causing me to jump out of my skin. When he took the entire thing in his mouth, I felt my knees buckle and reached up, grabbing ahold of his warm shoulders to support myself. "Like that, do you?" he whispered, moving to the other one to torture it as well as his hand drifted down, touching my belly, then the outside of my panties.

I stilled and he lifted his head, his eyes boring into mine. "I'll stop," he rasped, his expression tight. "I won't do this if you don't want to, Jess. Dammit, I'm not, it's not…"

My heart pounding, I hesitated for a moment, knowing that I probably should stop him. "I'm not looking for a quick fuck," I whispered, steeling my courage. "You need to know that."

"I know," he simply said, surprising me. His hands left my body as he pushed them through his hair, sending spray of water in all directions. He was as tight as a bowstring, yet he had stopped. Dipping into the water, I pushed my breasts back into my bra with trembling hands, my arousal still weighing heavily on my body. My body was in shambles, his touch shaking me to my very core and sending all sorts of questions flowing through my mind at why he was doing this, with me.

Kyle ducked under the water and disappeared for a moment, presumably to gain control as I was trying to do, before surfacing, giving me a long, heated look. "Let's go back to the boat."

I sighed loudly but didn't object as he guided us back to the ladder, climbing on board before helping me up and out of the water, handing me a white towel in the process. The sun was warm on my exposed skin as I watched him grab a beer out of the galley and take a large swig of it, nearly draining it in one gulp, tension evident in his face. I entered the galley as well, watching as his eyes lingered on the knotted towel around my body. "Kyle."

"Don't," he said harshly, putting the bottle on the table and grabbing another, the cap flying off. "I need a moment, Jess."

"I'm sorry," I said softly, watching as he finished that one as well in record pace.

"Don't be," he finally said, putting down the bottle before looking at me. "Hell, I don't deserve to be touching you this way. You are helping me out and I am damn near molesting you every chance I get." He then swore and rubbed a hand over his face, something akin to longing in his expression. "You deserve someone better than me."

My heart stopped as I took in his words, the look on his face. I couldn't believe that he was saying something like that to me when I was thinking the exact same thing about him. "It's not your fault, Kyle," I finally said, reaching up to cup his cheek. "I'm just as much to blame in this." I then reached up with my other hand, cradling his face between my hands. It was my favorite thing to do to him, to feel the warmth of his skin, the prickled stubble under my palms. I also felt the strength in him, his very life vibrating under my touch. "You are an awesome guy," I said softly, looking into his eyes. "Anyone would be lucky to have you."

Kyle closed his eyes for a moment and we just stood there, the sound of the water lapping around the boat the only noise for miles. He was awesome, I wasn't lying to him. Did I trust myself to take the next step with him? If I did, it was only a matter of time that I would lose myself as well. I was already in danger of doing that very thing.

Leaning in, I gave him a brief kiss on the lips, gasping as his arms went around me and he deepened the kiss. It wasn't a kiss of pleasure; it was pure, unadulterated passion as he ravaged my mouth in a way that I could feel it clear down to my toes. Our tongues danced and tiny shivers of passion shimmied down my body, making me acutely aware of my chest pressed up against his, his leg now wedged between mine. My body was on fire as he pulled away, his hands working furiously at the knot in the towel.

"I need you," he rasped, ripping the material away. "Please."

I could hear the desperation in his voice and felt the first seeds of emotion unfurling in my heart for him. I was going to lose my heart to him. "Okay," I heard myself say. "Okay."

Kyle's nostrils flared as he pulled me into the bedroom, sending me tumbling onto the bed as he loomed over me, an odd look on his face. "Why are you agreeing to this, Jess?" he asked, leaning over me until our foreheads touched.

A thousand answers ran through my brain, that all were discarded nearly immediately. Truthfully, I didn't know why but I knew he needed me, desperately, in more ways than one. So, I told him the truth. "You need me," I said softly, reaching up to touch his cheek. "And I need you. Isn't that enough?"

A shudder went through him as he backed away, his eyes roaming my body in a leisurely manner. "I will make this good for you, Jess."

"I have no doubt," I replied with a smile as his fingers trailed down my stomach to the waistband of my panties, still wet from the swim. His fingers danced over the cotton and I arched against his touch, knowing this was going to be quick and furious. Kyle hissed as he pushed them aside, touching my core with one, then two fingers.

"Kyle," I breathed, feeling his fingers slip across the sensitive nub, causing me to cry out as the first orgasm shattered me.

"Come for me," Kyle said, his fingers rubbing me over the edge.

"Kyle, oh dear God," I nearly squealed as the second overcame me, whimpering as his fingers disappeared.

"Shh, darling, I'm just getting ready," he said, the audible tear of a condom wrapper filling my ears. "God, you are gorgeous and so ready." The bed dipped as he loomed above me, his fingers interlacing with mine as he positioned himself. "Look at me," he said harshly, causing me to open my eyes.

"I see you," I said softly, arching against him. His grin was feral as he entered me, filling me to the core and causing me to gasp.

"You feel so good," he said just above my ear, his rhythm beginning to take shape. "I won't be lasting long, Jess."

"I'm. Coming. Again," I panted as he rocked against me over and over again. It was wonderful, it was hot, and I was being pushed over the edge rapidly.

"Say my name," he rasped in my ear, the bed beginning to squeak against our movements. "Please."

"Kyle," I said, locking eyes with him. "Kyle."

"Yes," he roared, picking up the tempo. I felt him pump harder and faster, my cries echoing his own as he came hard and fast.

My eyes never leaving his face, I watched as he enjoyed the throes of his orgasm, wordlessly watching this incredible man above me. Touching the sheen of sweat on his chest, I ran my hands over his shoulders and into his hair, not believing what had just transpired between us. It had been amazing and I couldn't tell if it was because I had waited so long or because I was with him.

He slowly pulled out and disposed of the condom before lying beside me, his breaths matching mine. We lay there for a few minutes as the boat rocked gently around us, not saying a word, not touching. Finally, Kyle propped up on an elbow, his blue eyes bright as his finger traced my cheek, then the upper swell of my breast, still encased in my bra.

"Well," I breathed, unsure of what to say, what to do. It definitely wasn't the time to freak out about sleeping with my boss. That would be much later, with alcohol. "At least it won't be awkward if your parents put us in the same room together."

Kyle chuckled, kissing my shoulder. "You are pretty awesome, you know that? All this time, under my nose."

"Yeah well, there was a reason," I retorted, giving him a dirty look. "I mean really your office can be a revolving door sometime. I mean how do you remember all of their names?"

"I don't," he shrugged, stretching out beside me. "I have no reason to. They want one thing and I give it to them. End of story."

A tiny silver of hope died inside me with his simple statement, the hope of me being different in his world going right out of the window. I had done the very thing I hadn't wanted to do, become just another face in his long line. "That's cold," I said gently, keeping the hurt out of my voice. I had entered this bed and I would deal with the consequences later.

"It's the truth," he replied, settling his arm around me, pulling me against his hard, warm body. "But I will tell you one thing, I've never brought one here. Never."

I sighed and melted against him, my fingers trailing over his chest in a mindless stroke. That had to mean something, to make me feel better about this whole thing.

***

I awoke sometime later, night all around me. The boat was swaying gently still, Kyle's front pressed up against my back, his arm draped over my middle. A cover had been pulled over us both and for a moment, I reveled in the fact that I was still in bed with the hottest man I knew, because he wanted me to be there. It was nice to be wrapped in someone's arms again, someone I barely knew yet knew well. There was a great deal to be worried about but in this one moment, I found myself smiling. This was definitely not what I had expected to happen when I had accepted his outing today.

Kyle shifted beside me and then groaned, turning over to push himself up off the bed. I flushed as I shamelessly looked at his body, barely visible in the dim moonlight. Holy hotness, his penis was huge.

A grin stole over his face as he stretched then yanked the covers off of me, the cool air assaulting my naked flesh just before he covered me with his body. "Tell me you are on the pill," he whispered, rubbing himself against me.

"I-I am," I rasped, the friction igniting my senses into overdrive.

"Good," he said as he entered me to the hilt, causing me to gasp at the difference of him without the condom. "I don't think you could feel any better than you do right now," he said, gripping my legs as I brought them around his waist.

I smiled as he rolled his hips, reaching up to touch his face, bringing him down for a soul-searing kiss. "Show me what you got."

"Yes ma'am," he smiled against my lips. I arched my body just right for him to slide in deeper. I moved with his thrusts, meeting him at every one, and he was the one who moaned low in his throat, gripping my legs tighter.

"Oh yes, Kyle," I urged as he took me higher and higher, the slow quiver of an orgasm building. One more thrust and I screamed out, causing him to bury himself harder and deeper, his hoarse cry following mine.

His body collapsed on mine as he shook, my hands going into his hair to hold him close. "Damn," he said, raising his head to look at me. "That was…"

"Pretty darn good," I finished, eliciting a grin out of him.

"You feel amazing around me right now," he whispered, his tongue grazing the shell of my ear before delving inside. "But I don't think I have anything left at this particular moment."

Laughing, I pushed at his shoulders until he rolled off me. I sat up on the bed as my head cleared from the haze of sex. Kyle sat up as well, reaching up to turn on a small lamp on the only piece of furniture in the room. In the dim light, I looked at him, taking in his sexy stubble on his jaw, the way the light bounced off his tanned skin.

"You are beautiful," I whispered, reaching out. He was and my heart ached at the sight. This was the man under the suit, the man that few rarely saw.

Kyle captured my hands and kissed my fingers, his other hand tangling itself in my hair. "I'm going to get something to drink. The bathroom is right through there."

Blushing, I watched as he strode out of the room into the galley, admiring his ass the entire way. What a thing of beauty. Sighing, I gathered up my tank top and underwear, finding a washcloth in the minuscule bathroom to clean myself up. I then eyed myself in the mirror, seeing a woman I didn't recognize staring back at me. There was a glow about me, my eyes sparkling in the light. I was a woman who had been very well fucked.

Grinning, I walked out to the galley, finding Kyle on his cell, a pensive look on his face. "Yes sir, I will be there in the morning. Thank you."

Pressing the end button, he looked up at me and I gave him a tentative smile, noticing that his expression had slipped back into the weary lawyer I knew him to be. "We've got to head back, don't we?"

"Yeah, that was the judge. My client has decided to waive his rights and plead guilty. I've got an emergency hearing in a few hours." He then rubbed a hand over his face, grabbing his shorts from the bench. Without so much as another word, he went above deck, the sound of the engines roaring to life. Rubbing my arms, I went back into the bedroom to dress.

Chapter 6

"I heard you sneaking in early this morning. Give me all the sordid details, now."

"I need coffee first," I grumbled at Gretchen, reaching for a mug. I had only slept maybe two hours since Kyle had dropped me off at my apartment. It had been a long, silent ride back, Kyle's mind obviously on his client and the case. It did sting a little when he didn't as much as touch me in any way, shape, or form, but I sucked it up, being the big girl that I knew I was going to have to be. At least that was what I was telling myself.

"OMG, you slept with him didn't you?"

I narrowed my eyes at Gretchen, who was sitting at the breakfast bar, her legs swinging back and forth like a child waiting for something exciting to happen. "I can see it on your face, you know. You might as well fess up."

"Okay, I did," I forced out, grimacing at the hot liquid as it slid down my throat. "Geez, I think you live for this kind of stuff."

"I can't believe you are banging the boss," Gretchen grinned, stretching her arms over her head. "Was he as good as we thought he was?"

I gave a tiny smile, knowing full well I wasn't about to spill my guts about the best sexual encounter I had experienced in my entire life. It was awesome and my body was feeling the effects of my little escapade. I would probably be feeling it for weeks.

"I knew it," Gretchen smiled, wagging her finger at me. "You lucky dog. When are you going to see him again? I hope you are going to draw the line at office sex. No offense, but I don't want to have to worry about finding you two going at it in his office."

"We have to spend time together next weekend," I replied with a frown. "We didn't make any plans otherwise."

"Well, maybe you already have him panting for more," Gretchen said, sliding off of the stool. I watched her walk back to her bedroom, the frown still on my face. Kyle hadn't made any plans with me, heck, I didn't even know of any plans in the near future. Crap, I was starting to feel like one of those women and I didn't like it. What had I gotten myself into?

***

A short while later, after a mind-clearing shower and fresh clothes, I headed uptown, intent to get my retail therapy in. I needed some new clothes for the trip next weekend, clothes that were befitting of being the girlfriend of a successful lawyer. It was apparent by his short words that I was going to struggle against his family anyway and I wanted to make a good impression, one that might get them to actually like their son. It was sad, I thought, as I looked through the racks of my favorite store. How could a family be like that to an obviously great person and hard worker just because he didn't fit into the mold they wanted him in?

Selecting a great pair of slacks and glitzy top off the sale rack, I paid for them and walked outside, enjoying the sunshine on this wonderful day. My stomach growled, reminding me that other than coffee, I hadn't eaten in quite a few hours and I stepped into one of my favorite delis, determined to take care of that problem. After collecting my sandwich and drink, I sat down at a corner table, pulling a paperback out of my purse. I didn't go anywhere without one because there was always a wait at least once a day.

The doorbell tinkled and I looked up, seeing Kyle's profile entering the deli as well, my heart going pitter-patter as I enjoyed the view of him in his court attire. I then did a double take and crouched down in my seat, realizing that he was not alone. A tall redhead stood with him, her attire not court-appointed by any means. Her sundress fit her body like a glove, showing off her tanned skin and long legs that seemed to never end. Together they made a striking pair and my stomach sunk at the sight. He was grinning at something she was saying and I felt my blood boil at the sight of her fingers on his shoulder, the same shoulder I had just bit only hours before.

"Dear lord," I muttered, pulling myself farther into the corner. I was turning into a jealous fanatic. There was no claim on him yet my declaration of not being a casual sex kind of girl obviously meant nothing to him. I shouldn't be surprised, yet I was hurt, far more hurt than I really should be. The redhead tittered with laughter as they waited to order, Kyle's face relaxed as I had seen it just twelve hours previously. He kept his hands by his side, but they were definitely friendly with each other, anyone could see that. I hunkered down in the corner and watched as they ordered their meals to go and walked out a short time later, never once spotting me. Sucking up the tears that threatened to cascade down my cheeks, I threw my food in the trash and exited. I had suddenly lost all appetite.

***

After another restless night, I procrastinated on even getting ready for work on Monday. It was bad enough that I would spend almost a week with him, alone, knowing that he had obviously enjoyed himself yesterday, from doing something pretty doggone amazing with me to the redhead. To have to sit in the office after that humiliation was killing me, but I was glad it was my secret humiliation. I didn't dare tell

Gretchen about the redhead and unless she was draped over his desk when we walked into the office, no one else was going to know that I had been dumped in a span of a mere twelve hours. Choosing black to match my mood, I threw on my clothes and walked to my car, driving at a snail's pace to delay the inevitable.

"Geez, you are moving like my grandma," Gretchen remarked as she met me at the elevator. "Are you still sore from your weekend fun?"

"Shove it, Gretch," I muttered, pressing the button.

"Wow, who peed in your cornflakes?" she asked, crossing her arms. "Spill it."

"I saw Kyle with another woman yesterday," I blurted out, surprised by the onslaught of tears in my throat. There went the idea of it being just my humiliation. "And not his grandmother."

"Oh geez," Gretchen said softly, pulling me into an awkward hug. "It's okay, Jess. Don't let him see that you even care about it. Sucks that you got to spend this week with him now. Do you want me to take him out? I need some practice at kickboxing anyway. He won't see it coming."

"No," I laughed, clearing my throat. "I'm being a ninny for even letting this bother me. It was just casual sex and there is nothing going on between us."

"Well, I can always spit in his coffee," Gretchen remarked as the doors opened and we stepped into the office. "Just let me know."

"Thanks," I said, grateful that I had a friend who had the potential to be violent on my behalf. Thankfully, Kyle's office was dark when we settled in and I threw myself into my work, trying to complete some things since I would be leaving for the rest of the week.

Around ten my inbox chimed and I opened the email, my face flushing as I read the contents. *What are you wearing?* it said. I looked at the sender and sighed, seeing Kyle's email as the sender. No doubt he was texting my email, as he did numerous times throughout the day when he needed something done.

None of your business, I typed back quickly. *Aren't you supposed to be paying attention in court?*

I am, came the reply a few moments later. *Waiting on the judge's ruling so I can come back to the office and see you. Is it see-through?*

I fought the urge to smile as I hovered over the delete icon, knowing that I shouldn't be bantering with him this way. I was supposed to be mad at him.

No, I finally typed back. It had to be easy for him to switch from one girl to the next, to have no feelings or regret for doing so.

Why don't you leave early today? the next email stated. *Meet me at the house for dinner. I still have yet to feed you appropriately.*

I bit my lip as I struggled to turn him down, knowing full well dinner wasn't the only thing on his mind. How he could want to sleep with me again after seeing the redhead was beyond my comprehension, but I wasn't going to allow him that chance, not tonight. *Sorry*, I wrote back. *Got to finish packing.*

When I got no reply, I felt a little let down that he didn't put up much of a fight to get me to accept. No doubt the redhead would be the next email he sent out. Grumbling, I pressed my palms to my eyes and forced the jealousy back to its hiding place deep within me. This was ridiculous. I was acting like I was in middle school and my boyfriend had cheated on me with the head cheerleader!

Turning back to my work, I concentrated on the case I was researching and not on my current sex with the boss issues.

Chapter 7

"Are you sure you want to do this? I mean you could back out now, Jess, and let him fend for himself."

"I will be fine," I smiled, hefting the suitcase in one hand. "Thanks for dropping me off, Gretch."

"Yeah well, smart move to meet at the airport," Gretchen replied, handing me my purse. "Less of a chance for a quickie before you left."

I rolled my eyes and shut the door, well aware of the airport security coming our way. "You better get out of here before you get a ticket," I said through the open window. "I will call you."

"Don't do anything I wouldn't do, oh wait, you already have!" Gretchen grinned, turning on the engine. "Have fun!"

I straightened and walked into the airport, taking a seat to wait for Kyle. Truth was, I wasn't so worried about the quickie. Okay, maybe I was and I was being chicken about spending time with him, alone. I hadn't seen him the rest of the day yesterday after turning down his offer for supper and had sent him an email stating I would meet him at the airport rather than have him come get me. I was afraid I would attack him at first opportunity as well, which didn't bode well for this trip. I could only hope that his parents were stuffy and insisted on separate bedrooms.

"Ready?"

I looked up and found Kyle standing over me, dressed down in a pair of jeans and green shirt, his sunglasses hooked into the buttons. His eyes drifted over me and I grew warm, nearly knocking him over as I stood. "Yes, let's go."

"First," he said, putting his bag down next to me. "I've been waiting to do this."

"What?" I asked before his arms went around me and his lips collided with mine, his kiss full of hunger and promises for later. I nearly melted against him as he slid his fingers into my hair and cradled my head, his tongue delving into my mouth. I grasped his shoulders in an effort not to slide to the floor, my body reacting to his closeness and touch in a way that I thought maybe we should go and do a quickie.

"I really wish you had come to the house," he whispered, rubbing his lips over mine. "We could have woken up together." He then looked down, his smile turning into a grimace as he took in my attire. "It's going to be a long, painful ride knowing you have that skirt on."

"And potentially no underwear," I smiled as he kissed me softly and drew away, collecting both of our bags in his hand and holding out the free one.

There had been a reason to wear the cute summer skirt and apparently it had worked.

"Come on, minx."

Putting my hand in his, I felt the turmoil of emotions as he interlinked our fingers and moved us to the desk to collect our tickets. Kyle was acting like we were picking up where we had left off yet I knew that I hadn't imagined the redhead nor the interaction in the deli. Had I misjudged that whole encounter? Why was he being so, so confusing? He was not a one-woman man, I knew that when I slept with him, but had something changed? Could I even dare to think that perhaps I could compete for this man's affections?

"You sure are deep in thought."

I turned toward Kyle, finding him watching me with those oh so sexy eyes and gave him a tentative smile, hoping that my emotions were not playing out live in my expressions. "I'm just nervous."

"Yeah, me too," he grinned, handing me my ticket. "But we will be fine, you will be fine. Come on, let's get this over with." We got through security without a cavity search and boarded the plane first, finding ourselves in first class to my surprise. "I find it hard to sit anywhere else," Kyle remarked as we sat in the two plush seats near the front of the plane. "Is this okay?"

"Okay?" I laughed, wiggling my feet out in front of me. "This is awesome."

"Good," he replied, bringing my hand up to kiss the back of it. "Too bad it's not a red-eye flight. We could possibly have some airplane fun in the dark."

"You never stop, do you?" I said with a grin, finding it very hard to stay upset with him. It would come up later, but for now, I could try and pretend that we were two adults, with no feelings involved.

"I try but it's very hard," he grinned back, leaning his head against the seat. I looked at his handsome profile, my heart doing a silly dance inside my chest and knew right then I was sunk, big time. There were feelings, lots of them.

***

The flight was uneventful, Kyle sleeping through most of it. I held tight to his hand as we soared above the clouds, afraid to let go lest he might disappear and I wake up from this dream. I was worried, so worried, about what I was experiencing and the hurt that was going to follow. It was only a matter of time before this fairytale ended and I was gorging myself on cookie dough and sappy romance novels. He and I, we just didn't mix in the real world, apart from this farce that we insisted on playing out. God, why had I slept with him?

Sighing, Kyle woke in time to depart, his roguish smile drawing out some of the turmoil that was currently going on inside of me. "I got a rental so we wouldn't have that awkward ride," he said as we collected our bags and headed into the sun. "And so we could make a quick exit if need be."

"Oh, it's not going to be that bad," I said as he led us to a sleek four-door vehicle in the rental lot. "I'm sure your family will be happy to see you."

Kyle stopped and looked at me, his mouth showing the strain of this reunion. "Don't think this is going to turn out roses and chocolate, Jess," he said, his fingers running through his hair. "My family will tolerate me and you because they have to. Then we will go our separate ways until the next wedding or funeral, whichever comes first. This isn't going to be a warm, cozy welcome."

He then let out a breath, his grin sliding back into place as I had seen it done numerous times before. "I'm glad you are agreeing to do this. It will make this week much more enjoyable."

"Yeah well, we will be sick of each other by then," I said lightly. "Don't worry, I will be by your side."

Kyle really smiled then, one that seemed to light up those beautiful eyes of his as he leaned down, dropping a kiss on my lips. "Thank you."

"No problem," I answered as he popped open the trunk and put our bags in. We climbed in and Kyle maneuvered the car onto the road with ease. The city soon faded in the distance as we passed through small, quaint towns, the kind that if you blinked, you missed it. We fell into a long silence, the tension in Kyle's body evident the farther we drove. I wanted to console him, but kept my hands to myself, instead looking out of the window for the most part.

At the next quaint little town, Kyle took a series of turns and I felt the tension build in the car as we ended up in a residential neighborhood with large colonial-style houses on the tree-lined street. It was the ideal American dream, and as we turned into a long, curved driveway, I couldn't help but think how our childhoods had differed. My parents, God bless them, were both government workers, civilians whose jobs caused us to move around a lot. Though they were loving and able to provide for me, we never really settled down in one place until I was much older. There hadn't been a childhood home such as this to go back to, there hadn't been lifelong friends to grow up with. I was not bitter in the least, yet wondered if Kyle realized how lucky he truly had been to have a permanent residence.

Pulling up behind an expensive-looking SUV, Kyle cut the engine and took a deep breath, his expression unreadable behind his sunglasses. "Listen, don't let them get to you," he said softly, his hands gripping the wheel. "Just be yourself and hope that this goes by fast."

Quelling my nervousness, I reached over and covered my hand with his, hoping that I could provide some comfort. "I will be here for you, Kyle. Don't worry, I got your back."

Kyle didn't answer as he pulled open the door and climbed out, coming around the front to open my door as well. Giving him the best smile I could, I climbed out, accepting his proffered arm.

"Come on," I said gently, looking at the imposing house in front of us with some trepidation. "Let's get this over with."

Kyle moved my hand down to his, interlacing our fingers and giving me a squeeze. "Let's go."

We started up the brick stairs to the double oak doors, pushing one of them open to gain entrance into a cool foyer. I fought the urge to smile as I noticed the same out of a magazine décor Kyle had in his home, wondering if they truly realized a house was to be cozy, not sterile. A large open living room was off to one side, the furniture light colored and not a piece of anything out of place.

"Kyle, you finally made it." A slim woman stood behind a wingback chair, her hair the same color as Kyle's. She had a cool expression on her perfectly sculpted features, her lips drawn into a flat line as she acknowledged our presence. I took in her straight out of J.Crew catalog clothing and suppressed the urge to tuck tail and run, realizing exactly what Kyle was trying to warn me about. There was nothing warm about this woman, nothing at all.

"Mother," Kyle said coolly, pulling me more into the room. "You are looking well."

"Is this her?" his mother replied, ignoring him as she gazed at me.

"This is Jessica," Kyle said, pulling me into the crook of his arm. "Jessica, this is my mother, Julia." I was grateful for his touch as his mother came closer, her mouth growing flatter by the moment as she took in my attire. It was obvious I was not the woman she would pick out.

"Well, welcome to our home, Jessica. I trust you will have a pleasant stay here." Not I hope, but I trust, which was no doubt the way she ran her household. I was growing more worried by the moment. "Your father should be home in a few hours," she continued, turning back to her son. "Your sister is coming for dinner at six. I put you in your bedroom. I trust you staying in the same room won't be a problem?"

"Not at all," Kyle replied, dropping his arm to grab my hand. "We will go get ready then."

Without another word, he dragged me out of the room and up a grand staircase to the second floor, where a long hallway full of doors greeted us, our footsteps making marks in the plush carpeting. I followed him helplessly as he pushed open one of the doors and propelled us inside, shutting the door firmly behind us.

"Wow," I breathed as he let go of my hand. "I have never seen something make you haul tail before."

"Sorry," he shrugged, his hands on his hips. "You have to take my mother in small doses. The longer you are in her company, the worse she tends to be."

"She seemed… nice," I forced out, looking around the room. It was a large bedroom, decorated like the rest of the house in mundane color palettes. A four-poster king bed dominated much of the room, with matching armoire and dresser completing the suite. An open door lay opposite of the bed, revealing a moderate-sized en suite bathroom.

"Looks like mother decided to redecorate," he replied as he took in the bedroom as well. "I bet my junk is in the basement."

"When is the last time you visited?" I asked, pulling the curtains aside to view a well-manicured backyard.

"Not since I graduated college," he replied, stunning me. Though we lived in separate states, I at least saw my family two times a year regardless. That had to be at least ten years given the fact I knew he was approaching thirty-five.

I heard him come up behind me, his hands sliding around my waist and pulling me against his body, immediately surrounding me in warmth. "You know there is a hot tub down there," he said softly, nibbling on my earlobe. "And I plan to enjoy it at some point this weekend, with you."

"I think your mother would object," I replied softly, gasping as his tongue traced the outer shell of my ear.

"I don't give a damn," he growled. His hands pulled my shirt out of my skirt, his fingers touching my bare skin, caressing my stomach before inching upward, brushing my already taunt nipples as his hands covered my breasts.

"Kyle," I breathed as molten lava coursed through my veins at his touch, the way he was trailing hot kisses down my neck.

"I want you," he breathed into my ear. "So fucking bad." He pushed himself against me, his arousal evident as I arched against him. I was wet, my body alive with painful need. Kyle growled low in his throat as he removed his hands, wrenching my skirt up around my hips and forcing me to step out of my panties. "Grab the windowsill."

Shaking, I grabbed the thin piece of wood at the bottom of the window as I heard the telltale sound of his belt unbuckling, his zipper sliding down before he entered me from behind in one full thrust. "Dear God," I moaned as he stretched and filled me, forcing me to grip the windowsill as my legs buckled.

"Yes," he echoed as he pulled back and thrust again, shattering my very core. The orgasm was overwhelming as Kyle picked up the tempo, me rocking back to match his thrusts. "That's it, Jess," Kyle coached, his voice strained. "Beautiful."

I moaned again as the orgasms started to build, one right after the other in waves. I squelched a scream as an explosion of light flashed before my eyes, followed by Kyle's convulsion inside me as we collapsed in a heap on the floor. I breathed in the fresh scent of clean carpet under my nose, my breath coming in short gasps as Kyle's weight shifted off of me. He flopped down on the floor next to me.

"Damn."

I couldn't find my voice to agree with his wording as I pushed myself up off the floor, my legs still wobbly from the aftershocks. Kyle reached out and gripped my ankle, his large hands sliding up my calf deliciously. "Where do you think you are going?"

Chapter 8

An hour later I straightened my skirt and slid on my flats, walking across the room where Kyle was buttoning up his shirt over that gorgeous chest of his. "Let me," I said softly, pushing his hands away. "I was beginning to think we weren't going to make dinner."

"If I knew we could get away with it, I would be taking that skirt off," he replied as I pushed the buttons through the holes, a shiver slicing through me as he cupped my cheek.

"Come on, bad boy," I smiled, removing his hand to place it in mine. "It's showtime." I turned toward the door and Kyle pulled me back against him, taking my hands in his.

"Listen, Jess," he began, his eyes growing soft as he searched mine. "I just wanted to thank you for doing this with me. I can't think of anyone else that could handle it as well as you are nor would I want anyone else by my side."

"Don't worry," I said, giving him a soft kiss on the lips. "I won't embarrass you. I've been dealing with you for years. Your family won't be that difficult." Kyle let out a strangled laugh and released me, pulling me toward the door.

I rolled my eyes as I allowed him to drag me down the stairs, my heart giddy in my chest. He had given me slow, sweet torture on the floor, the bed, and in the shower since we had arrived in his bedroom a few hours ago, so much that I knew I would ache in the morning from all of this extracurricular activity. There had been no words yet I could feel through his touch, knowing I was losing every inch of my heart with each one. We had explored each other lazily during that time and I felt comfortable under his intense gaze, no secrets left between us. I knew him more intimately than anyone else and even so, I knew he wouldn't be mine in the long run.

Kyle guided us to the dining room, where a long table laden with delicate china was already set up. Everyone was already seated when we entered, rising as Kyle drew up short.

"Son," a large, bulky man with salt and pepper hair acknowledged Kyle from the head of the table.

"Father," Kyle said evenly, pulling me into the enclosure of his arms. I could feel the tension in his grasp and tried to put on the bravest smile I could muster. "This is Jessica. Jessica, this is my father Brent, my sister Nicole, and her fiancé Reese."

I smiled at the dark-haired woman who resembled Kyle with her features, sitting next to a man who could be described as an all American football type jock with slick blond hair and a warm expression that immediately made me feel at least like I had an ally in the room. Kyle's sister nodded in my direction, a small smile on her face as she looked me over in the circle of her brother's arms.

"And you remember Danielle, Kyle." His mother smiled, nodding to the redhead at the end of the table.

Kyle's arms dropped immediately as I felt him stiffen, then my own body react jealousy as I recognized her as being the same woman I had seen him with a few days prior. It was like a cold dunking when you least expected it.

"Kyle," she purred, her cultured voice matching the perfection of her makeup and clothing. "So good to see you again."

"Danielle," Kyle said flatly.

"Danielle is staying with us for the wedding," Julia replied, looking at the woman warmly. "She is between assignments right now."

"I am a flight attendant," Danielle explained, apparently to just me since everyone else in the room must be aware of her job. "My next turn is in Europe next week."

Kyle said nothing as he motioned for us to sit, me beside his sister and he beside Danielle. I tried my best to keep my smile as I noted the seating arrangement and the exchange passed between Kyle's parents as they viewed their son and Danielle together. It was obvious she was their choice for their son. Hell, I wasn't who I would have chosen for their son. The question was still up in the air on why they had been together just a few days ago, given his reaction to her.

Thankfully, the food came out just as we sat down, which limited conversation. "So what do you do, Jessica?" Nicole asked as we delved into our salads.

"I, uh, work in Kyle's office," I choked out, receiving an arched eyebrow from Julia in the process.

"Interdepartmental relationship, huh," Brent barked out, his fork hovering near his mouth. "I am surprised you allow that, son."

"Kyle is a wonderful lawyer," I interrupted, feeling the need to stick up for him. "I am very blessed to be working for such a talented person."

"Thank you," Nicole said softly enough for my ears only. Surprised, I looked up to find her gazing at her brother adoringly, seeing her in a new light. It appeared not everyone in the family thought the same.

"You can't stop true love," Kyle finally answered, his warm gaze on me. "Jess is a valuable asset not only in my office, but in my life as well. I don't know what I would do without her."

I blushed at his comments, knowing that I shouldn't let them affect me too deeply. After all, we were putting on an act, regardless of what we were doing on the side.

"Bravo," Danielle remarked, giving two soft claps as she held up her wineglass. "Here's to true love and wedded bliss. May I be lucky enough to find it one day." I held up my glass and tipped it, careful to only take a small sip of the sweet wine, remembering my embarrassment with Kyle over too much wine. I had no desire to have a repeat performance of that night.

The rest of the dinner was surprisingly quiet and before long, we were retiring to the backyard, where Julia was showing off the area where her daughter would wed.

"You know this isn't my preferred place to do this," Nicole remarked as we stood on the patio, watching from above. "I wanted to do the beach, but mother wouldn't hear of it."

"It's your wedding," I replied, my thoughts straying to crazy ideas of Kyle and me barefooted on the beach. "Why not do what you want to do?"

"You can't do that with mother," Nicole sighed, clasping her hands in front of her. "I'm sure Kyle has told you. Mother likes it her way and her way only. That is why he hasn't been back to this house in so long. He was able to escape, I wasn't." She then turned toward me, taking my hands in hers. "I really, really hope you love my brother," she said softly, her eyes reminiscent of the ones I now adored. "I hope you can provide what he hasn't gotten from our family. He seems happy, happier than I have ever seen him."

I gave her a small smile, my heart in torment over what this girl was thinking and what was truly going on between her brother and me. I knew what I was feeling and what I had felt over the last few chaotic days. I was falling hard for the man that had turned my life upside down, the man that I wanted to stick up for, the man I wanted to selfishly keep as my own. It wasn't possible. No, there would be one-sided feelings on this.

Sighing, I watched as he carried on a conversation with Reese, a little more relaxed as they shared a laugh. "Get him away from this place," Nicole added, dropping my hands. "You already protect him, I can't ask for much more."

***

"Well, that wasn't too bad," Kyle remarked as he closed the door to the bedroom. "Mother was well, she was herself."

"Kyle," I began with a deep breath. "Who is Danielle?"

"Danielle?" he asked, shrugging out of his shirt. "She's a family friend. We went to school together."

"Were you ever involved?" I squeaked out, my mouth going dry at the sight of his bare chest.

Kyle sighed and crossed the room, gathering me into his arms. "Don't worry about her," he said softly, his hand going into my hair. "She's not even on that level with me anymore."

"I'm not worried," I said shakily, pulling out of his embrace. "We are pretending to be together, right?"

Kyle's lower jaw ticked as his expression became hard and he thrust his hand through his hair, causing me to swallow in return. "Right," he finally ground out, throwing on his shirt as he opened the door. "I'm going out."

I jumped as he slammed the door shut, the paintings on the wall rattling in return, wondering what had just happened. I had only spoken the truth yet he acted like it was something else, something that I was feeling as well. Could it be possible? Did I even dare hope?

Hours passed without his return as I took a hot shower and climbed into bed, staring at the clock as it ticked slowly by. Finally, as I was starting to drift off to sleep, Kyle stumbled in the door, easing it shut. I froze as I heard his shoes hit the floor, then his pants before he climbed into bed, reaching over to touch my bare arm with his fingers. I could smell the alcohol on his breath but didn't move as those long fingers drifted over my shoulder then to touch the tresses on my pillow. I closed my eyes tightly against the soft touch, wanting desperately to turn over and take him into my arms.

"God, I wish you knew," he said softly, startling me out of my thoughts. He then sighed heavily, pressing a soft kiss on my shoulder before rolling over. I lay there frozen as his snores filled the air, wondering what the hell he was talking about.

Chapter 9

The next morning came all too soon. I awoke to an empty bed, the sound of the shower running in the bathroom alerting me that I was indeed not in a dream, but tortuous reality. Throwing back the covers, I padded to the bathroom, shedding my clothes in the process. Kyle was standing away from the curtain, his arm braced against the wall, his face lifted upward to the water as I climbed in, my hands brushing the muscles of his back softly before I wrapped my arms around his lean waist.

"I'm sorry," I said softly, pressing a kiss to his back. "I know this is difficult for you and I shouldn't be adding to it."

He shuddered and turned in my arms, kissing me hard on the lips. "I'm sorry I roped you into this."

"You didn't force me," I replied with a small smile, touching his chest with my hands. "Just like anything else, you aren't forcing me."

He then gave a small groan as I took his flat nipple into my mouth, swirling my tongue around it. "Jesus," he whispered, his hands in my hair.

"Relax," I said, pulling back, desire swirling in my veins. Holy hotness, he was perfect and I wanted to have him trembling under my touch for once. "Let

86

me take care of you." Kneeling before him, I touched him, already hard and ready for me. "It's beautiful," I said honestly, taking him fully into my palm, feeling its length before touching the tip of it with my lips in a soft kiss.

"Jess," he said in a strangled voice, his hands clenching in my hair. "You don't... damn."

"Shh," I whispered, the water dripping all around me as I took him fully into my mouth. I worked it slow, ramping up my speed until he was groaning and attempting to pull away from my mouth. Grabbing his ass, I pulled him back and before long he stiffened, his harsh cry echoing in the shower as I finished him off. I leaned back and wiped my lips, pulling myself back against the length of him, seeing the drained look on his handsome face.

"Good God, Jess," he said softly, his sexy grin sliding back into place. "That is an awesome way to start a morning."

"Good morning," I replied with a smile as he took my face in his hands, his eyes tender as he searched mine.

"A damn good morning," he echoed, rubbing his nose with mine.

I sighed as I enjoyed the tender touch, kissing his thumb as it drifted over my swollen lips. I was sunk, big time. Nicole had hit the nail on the head. I loved this man.

We stayed in the shower until the water grew cold, running us out and forcing us to start another trying day. Kyle's grip was tight on my hand as we descended the stairs, pausing as we saw the crowd gathered at the bottom.

"Golf and shopping," Nicole announced, seeing us on the stairs. "You can guess which one you are going to do."

"Great," Kyle muttered under his breath as he pulled me to him. "Don't let them get you flustered," he whispered in my ear, his fingers briefly touching my cheek.

"Don't forget to hide their bodies if you decide to take them out," I added with a smile, earning a chuckle from him. My heart fluttered as he kissed me gently in front of everyone, lingering for a moment.

"Here," he said, pulling out his wallet to hand me his credit card.

"Oh no," I protested, handing it back to him. "I've got my own money."

"I know," he said, tucking a lock of hair behind my ear, his grin sinful. "Buy something racy. It will be money well spent." He then kissed me again, tucking the card into my front pocket before joining the men, who were on their way out.

"Wow. That was so not the brother I am used to seeing," Nicole remarked as I all but floated down to her side. "Whatever you are doing to him, Jessica, keep it up."

"Yeah, well, I'll try," I responded, my cheeks flushing. "Where are we going?"

***

"Geez," I whistled, dropping the price tag as if it had burned me. "Did you see how much that underwear is?"

"Get them," Nicole laughed. "It's not like my brother can't afford them."

"Dear lord," I muttered, moving well away from the rack. We were in a ritzy mall in the neighboring town, the car ride definitely strained with little to say. I was lost in my own thoughts of Kyle and what was transpiring between us, the soft feelings that were starting to compound at least on my end. Julia and Danielle were sticking together, apparently having more in common than with the two of us anyway. "Are you excited about your wedding?"

"I am," Nicole smiled, two bright spots appearing on her cheeks. "I can't wait to be Mrs. Barnten. Reese and I have been together ten years now and it's past time that we make it official." She then turned to me, her eyes glittering like blue sapphires. "I don't care about getting married in the backyard. I don't care that my dress weighs thirty pounds or that I wanted chicken wings instead of the grilled chicken my mom insisted on. What matters is that I am marrying my best friend, the man that I love more than life itself."

"I envy you then," I said, a lump in my throat. "And I am glad that you are not your mother or Danielle. Kyle had me super worried."

"I am far from my mother," she laughed. "As for Danielle, she believes that she is to be Kyle's wife. I don't want to scare you off in any way, but her parents and my parents have planned their union since birth. Danielle and Kyle have been forced together more times than you realize and each time he has shied away." She then sighed, concern etched on her face. "I think that is why he left as soon as he could, moved away to be rid of my parents' overbearing demeanor. He doesn't want to marry her any more than he wants to move back home."

I smiled through gritted teeth, knowing that there had to be more than what Kyle had expressed the night before when I had brought up Danielle. Great, a tall model redhead was my competition now at least. Once we got home, it would be any woman in a twenty-mile radius. My chances of being able to hold onto him were dimming by the moment.

"Come on," Nicole interrupted, linking arms with me. "Let's go find the evil twins. I'm sure they are plotting another wedding at this moment."

***

We found the two in one of the restaurants that flanked the mall, sipping on their wine and tapping their manicured nails against the table as we slid into the booth.

"Well, well, don't you both look as if you have made friends," Danielle remarked, her green eyes assessing me.

"I hope Nicole didn't tell too many secrets about the family," Julia remarked, looking at her daughter. "Tell me, Jessica. What do you think about my son?"

"Kyle is wonderful," I replied, meeting her eye. "He's the best thing that has ever happened to me." And that wasn't a lie; he was truly the best thing in a long time. "And he's very successful in his practice. I am sure you are so proud of what he has accomplished."

"Yes, well, he's cutthroat just like his father," Julia sniffed. "Danielle, did you get a chance to visit him?"

"We had lunch," Danielle said, a cat-like smile on her face. "You know, catch up on old times. Why not once did he mention you, Jessica? I find it very interesting with all of this display of affection now."

"You know how private Kyle can be," I fired back, giving her a sweet smile. I could play bitch as well; Gretchen had taught me how to be nice nasty. "It must be nice to catch up with old friends." Danielle's façade broke, allowing me to see the plotting woman underneath for a moment, knowing full well I would have to watch my back the rest of the weekend.

"Yes, well, Danielle knows Kyle better than anyone," Julia replied, patting the younger woman's hand. "But we are glad to have you to share this excitement this weekend, Jessica."

"Yes we are," Nicole chimed in, her smile the only real one at the table. Gah, no wonder Kyle hadn't visited this woman in a while. It was going to be hard enough to stomach her fakeness this weekend and I was glad my turn with her would be done. I almost could feel sorry for the girl that Kyle would ultimately call his wife as she would have this dragon of a mother-in-law to deal with. My chest ached at the thought, but I shrugged it off, knowing that it was going to come sooner or later. We had really good sex and I could almost say we had become good friends, but that's where it stopped. Though I had true feelings for him on my end, I wasn't expecting to have them returned to me. I would give him everything I could in the meantime and at least at the end of this adventure, he would have felt love. It was apparent it wasn't coming from the woman across the table.

How sad, I thought as Nicole handed me a menu. No wonder Kyle had thrown out all kinds of warnings before we got here. I wasn't finding anything warm or exciting about his parents at all.

Chapter 10

"He's not destined for the likes of you."

Taking a deep breath, I turned around and faced Julia, who was giving me her best I hate you stare. Now I knew where Kyle had gotten his glares from. "Excuse me?"

"You are not going to be my daughter-in-law."

"Ma'am, Kyle and I haven't even talked about marriage yet but I am sure if that happens, you will be the first one to know," I replied, crossing my arms over my chest. I had walked out onto the back deck while Kyle napped in the room, his golf trip seemingly as successful as my shopping trip had been. Neither one of us really wanted to talk about it. The look on his face when he had gotten back told me what I needed to know. My heart ached at what he had endured living with the woman before me, how it had affected his current lifestyle.

"Do not get smart with me," Julia fired back. "You, you are nothing but a diversion for him. He will marry someone of his stature."

"I wish you knew your son," I said softly, determined not to stoop to her level. "He's a great guy, a great lawyer. He's well respected and awesome to be around. I am sorry you don't see the reason to be happy for him."

Julia gave me one hard look and I inwardly cringed, waiting for her blast once more. Instead, a glimmer of tears caught my eye as she hastily blinked them away, rubbing her arms with her hands. "You love him, don't you?"

"I…" I started, confused at this turn of events. "Yes, I love him very much." And I did. I loved him more with every passing day and the thought terrified me.

"I can hear it in your voice, see it in your eyes when you talk about him. I've failed him, we've failed him and I am surprised he's still speaking to us." She then moved toward the railing, where I had been standing. "We had such high hopes for him. He's his father's son, strong willed and hard headed. We tried to keep him close, but only succeeded in pushing him farther away. It's always been our dream to see him marry Danielle, live right down the street and follow in his father's footsteps. Now, now I can't even get him to answer my phone calls."

As I listened to her, I couldn't help but feel somewhat sorry for what she was going through as well. This was a new turn of events from the woman who had been so harsh earlier. "Listen, I'm sure Kyle doesn't hate you," I lied, looking at her. "Perhaps if you just spent some time with him then you could talk."

"It's too late for us," she replied with a long sigh. "But it does make me happy that you will be there to take care of him in my absence."

I gave her a faint smile, now hating the fact that we were lying to her. She only wanted the best for her son, just struggled on how to show it to him. If neither one of them ever budged on their stance, however, they would never get any kind of reconciliation going. "Your son needs to understand why he gets nothing but bitterness from you," I finally said, pushing away from the railing and moving back toward the door. "And I'm not going to be the one to do that, you need to be. If you value any future with your son, with his wife, or any future grandkids, I would work out the differences now." As soon as I said it, I realized I hadn't inserted me in there, but his wife, which wouldn't be me.

Julia gave me a long, hard look and I held my breath for the onslaught of questions that were sure to follow. "If my son is as smart as I think he is, he won't let you go, Jessica," she finally said, though a tiny part of me knew that she knew that this wasn't a conventional relationship. Parents were not born yesterday. "I hope that you will fight for him in the instance."

"All I can guarantee is that right now, he is loved," I said softly, meeting her stare. There was no need to lie to her anymore nor was I scared of what she thought. "Even if he never knows it."

"I understand," she answered, giving me a grim smile, understanding the words that I veiled in that one statement. "And if you need anything…"

"I will be fine," I interrupted, holding up my hand. I didn't want her sympathy for what was going to happen with this relationship, but I didn't get the impression that she was upset that we had deceived her.

"I am sure you will," she finally said. "Good night, Jessica."

"Good night," I answered and escaped into the house before I started bawling in her presence. What a mess, what a hot, holy mess.

***

"Come back here, we aren't done yet."

I giggled as Kyle grabbed ahold of my wrist and pulled me toward him, causing me to snuggle against his hard chest once more. Not that I was complaining. At this point, I couldn't think of anywhere else I would rather be. "They are going to think we are avoiding them, Kyle."

"I am avoiding them," he said, his hand drifting into my hair. "I would much rather spend the day in bed with you then to be forced to spend it where I am not wanted."

"But it's your family," I protested softly, feeling the heat of him against my cheek. My body was sated, my heart nearly bursting from the tender lovemaking we had just experienced and I didn't care to leave the bed either, afraid that this bright spot in my life would be over and done with. I drifted my fingers over his bare stomach lightly, receiving a satisfied grunt in response. "Besides, the bluegrass festival starts this evening and I want to eat something horribly bad for me tonight. Maybe a greasy deep-fried something."

Kyle's chest shook with laughter and I slapped his abs, knowing exactly what he was thinking and it had nothing to do with food. "Come here." He grabbed my arm and pulled me against him, all of his hard body fitting into my soft one, sending a shaft of heat shooting through my body. Gah, I didn't think I would ever get tired of him if he was mine all the time. "I will get you whatever you want," he grinned, kissing the tip of my nose. "As long as you wear something short and easy accessible."

"I don't know how I am going to keep up with you," I sighed as his fingers drifted over my shoulder and down the middle of my back. "You are going to wear me out with all of this sex."

"Just as long as it's me," he said, some of his easy grin sliding into something more serious.

"Of course," I smiled, pushing at him lightly before moving out of his reach. "Besides you keep me in bed enough of the day already. I don't have time for anyone else." He chuckled and released me, allowing me to climb out of the bed and move into the bathroom, closing the door behind me. I cut on the shower and leaned against the door, hating the way I was feeling about this and the easy ways I was falling into a pattern with him, becoming more and more comfortable in his presence. Staying in this comfort zone with him wasn't going to be an option after we finished out this weekend, it was never part of the plan to begin with. The question was, how was I going to be able to walk away?

***

"You look beautiful, Nicole. I would die for a body like yours."

"You look great as well, Jess. That green is gorgeous on you." I smiled as I looked down at the green strapless I had brought, glad that Gretchen had thrown it in the suitcase at the last minute. Kyle's hungry gaze had been enough for me to silently thank my best friend.

The night was warm and perfect for a night at the square, Nicole and I walking side by side as the guys walked ahead of us. My heart jolted at the sight of Kyle's lean profile in the streetlight, the way he joked with Reese as we walked down the street. His parents had declined to walk with us and for once I was grateful, though my perception of them had changed. It wasn't my place to try and mend the fences between them and Kyle, but I was glad that I understood both sides now.

"You know we will be expecting your invite in the mail by next year," Nicole said, hooking her arm with mine. "By the looks of it, I would say a ring will be coming soon."

"I wouldn't bet on it," I muttered, dismissing the notion about any sparkling diamond in my future. I wouldn't even entertain those thoughts. Hell, we were sleeping together, but that was it. There was no relationship, no sharing of tender feelings. I loved him yes, but he hadn't alluded to anything other than the favor I was returning to him and the satisfied kisses after the hottest sex imaginable. But just the tiny bit of hope flared in my chest at the thought of this continuing, that this could become something serious. Could I really compete with all of those women back home? Could I be enough for him?

Tuning out my thoughts, I saw that the entire downtown had been lit up with lights of all kinds, the strains of bluegrass music intermingling with laughter from the people around us. Vendors lined the street as we joined the crowd, the tantalizing smells of barbeque, hamburgers, and chicken causing my stomach to rumble appreciatively.

"Welcome to Friday night on the square," Nicole smirked as we stopped in the midst of it all, reaching the Reese and Kyle. "And our joint semi last night as single people group."

"Oh my God," I exclaimed, stopping in my tracks. "Why didn't you tell me? This is so not what a bachelorette should be." Not that I had been to many, but I had seen the parties on TV. They involved flashing buttons, hot guys, and lots of alcohol. Besides I assumed that she had already had one. Only a fool would have it the night before their marriage.

"No, no, it's fine really," she laughed, grabbing my arm. "We didn't want to have to go through the hoopla of the traditional marriage festivities, like parties and the like. This will be all of it rolled into one."

"But what about your friends?" I asked. If I ever did walk down the aisle I would want Gretch at my side before the wedding. So far, I had seen not one member of the bridal party.

"We didn't want a big bridal party so we ditched those too," she said sheepishly. "Mom put up a fuss of course but my closest friends will be here in the morning. You will be wishing you never asked. They were all in love with my brother in high school."

I smiled then, glad that I wouldn't have to be pulling anyone's hair out over Kyle tonight. Gah, there I go again. I was being overly obsessed with my boss but hey, I knew what he looked like naked. There was no way I was going to share that with anyone else. Kyle's smile nearly knocked me down as I reached him, casually sliding my hand into his and grinning like a fool when he squeezed back. This was more than showing off in front of his family. We had them in our back pockets with our fake relationship.

"So let me show you around before dinner."

"You got thirty minutes!" Nicole exclaimed as we walked away.

"Don't make us late or she will never forgive us," I replied as we strolled down the middle of the street among the crowd. "What's all of this about anyway?"

"First of the month block party," Kyle explained, nodding to nearly everyone we passed. "It's tradition. We come out of our big homes and mingle like real people for at least one night. Everyone gets drunk and then we go home to do it all over again the next month."

"A drunk fest, awesome," I smiled.

"I remember the last time you got good and wasted," he teased, pulling me against his side, wrapping his arm around my waist. "And you survived a night, in my bed, with your clothes on."

"Don't remind me," I groaned, remembering my botched wine-induced night. I knew his toilet very, very well.

"Well, next time the results will hopefully be better," he said softly.

I stopped dead in my tracks and looked at him, my heart in my throat. "What?" he asked, his brow furrowed.

"This, this thing between us, what is it to you?" I asked softly, my hands smoothing the imaginary wrinkles on his shirt. I was well vested in this relationship, probably more than I should be, but what he felt, I didn't know. I was scared to know.

"Well, we have some amazing sex," he grinned, some of my hope fleeing out of the window. Yeah, exactly what I was afraid of.

"Well, I am glad you didn't pick Shirley," I finally said, taking the hurt out of my voice. What was I expecting? This wasn't even a real relationship. I signed up for this, I took my panties off one leg at a time every step of the way.

"Yeah, me neither," he smiled, putting a finger under my chin and forcing me to meet his gaze. "Hey, are we okay?"

"Just fine," I gave him a false smile and quickly averted my eyes before he could see any of the emotion in them. "Come on, show me this one-street town before dinner."

***

Thirty minutes later, we walked into the restaurant right behind the soon to be married couple to shouts of "surprise" as the lights came on in a cozy little Italian place off the main thoroughfare, packed to the gills with smiling faces that looked equally excited to see the couple.

"Oh my God," Nicole exclaimed as Reese hugged her close. "This was... I wasn't expecting this..."

"Exactly," Reese finished for her, a smile on his face. "Surprise, love. I know you said you didn't want a rehearsal dinner, but your friends wouldn't let it go. They insisted on throwing you a surprise rehearsal party so here we are."

"I'm glad you did," Nicole exclaimed happily, kissing him on the lips. A group of women immediately surrounded her as they moved deeper into the restaurant, their eyes straying to us. Great, the ones I had been warned about a day early.

Julia and Brent also appeared, though they made no move to embrace anyone in particular. I did catch the faint nod she sent my way, glad to see that I didn't dream up our little talk. Another older couple approached and I could tell immediately that it was

Reese's parents. The resemblance was striking between him and his father.

"Ah, the other happy couple. So glad you could make it. Love your dress, Jessica, it flatters your figure so well."

Danielle's voice drifted over me and I forced a smile on my face as I turned toward her voice. Barf, I wanted to jump across the room and scratch her eyes out. Apparently, her claws were out to play as I surveyed Danielle's skin-tight red dress that barely covered her you know what, the V-neckline just barely above being slutty. While most redheads would stay away from the color, she had embraced it, completing the look with red lipstick and black pumps that could not be comfortable. "Danielle, how nice of you to say that. It's nothing compared to your dress though."

She gave me a false smile and sidled up to Kyle, who either was not seeing the show before him or choosing to ignore it. "Kyle, daddy wants to see you for a second. You don't mind, Jess?"

"Not at all," I said through clenched teeth as she dragged him away. Kyle gave me a grin and allowed Danielle to pull him away into the crowd, leaving me to move aside lest the giggling crowd of girls run me down. "Be right back." Yeah, sure, I knew what she was thinking. Territorial flags went up in my head but I shrugged them away. There was no reason for me to act like this, no reason whatsoever. I might be in love with the man, but this wasn't a real relationship, this wasn't anything that would go beyond our plane ride back to Texas.

***

"I know what is really going on here."

I sighed as I recognized Danielle's haughty voice, wondering if the night was going to get any stranger. Kyle had deposited me at this table an hour ago before being pulled away by one person or another, the entire town trying to reconnect with him. I had watched him laugh and shake hands with nearly everyone in the room, like a politician on election night. Not once had he attempted to introduce me, which was fine. It wasn't like I was ever going to see these people again anyway. I should be thinking about my future, my next job instead of Kyle's killer grin and beautiful chest under his shirt. "What would that be?"

"I know the truth," Danielle smiled as she came into my view, sliding into the seat in front of me. "I know you and Kyle are not the lovey-dovey you are putting on for the rest of these people. He didn't mention you at all on my last visit. I didn't see any of your stuff at his house nor did I get the vibe from him that he was involved with anyone."

"I'm sure snooping around someone's private property is against the law," I replied, taking a sip of my water.

"You know, Jessica, you are not as smart as you hope you are," she said, looking at her fingernails. "I see the way you look at him, the hope in your eyes. Honey, I am here to tell you that Kyle will never say the 'L' word to you. He will never choose anything over that precious job of his and the fun he can have by staying unattached." She then shot a searing look in my direction, dropping her voice dangerously low. "I know firsthand. I loved that man more than anything. I followed him to Texas, gave him my virginity and my heart. I held onto the hope that he was going to put a ring on my finger straight out of law school. Instead, I got the boot, just like every other woman in his life. Don't think that whatever you are trying to pull will stick when you leave."

"If you know so much about him, why did you stay all those years?" I asked, unaffected by her rant. She sounded like a wounded ex-girlfriend to me and wasn't telling me anything I wasn't either already aware of or prepared for. I knew his love life was a revolving door, I knew that he wasn't serious about anyone or anything other than his job. I had worked for him long enough to know better, though a small piece of me, a very small piece, thought something might be different this time.

"I loved him," she said softly, some of the fight leaving her face. Instead, I saw a mirror image of me in a week or so and hated what I was seeing. "Listen, I know I haven't been the best person to you in the last few days, but I am going to tell you straight up what I have experienced. Get out and don't hang on to what might be. It didn't work for me and all you end up with is a shattered heart and wasted time on something that was never going to happen in the first place." She then slid back into her smile, one that didn't quite reach her eyes as she stood, adjusting the hem of her dress in the process. "This does not mean we are friends by any means, I hope you know that."

"I appreciate your honesty," I told her as she turned to go. She nodded tightly and disappeared into the crowd, leaving me with my water and not much else.

Chapter 11

"Reese looks nervous. They have been together ten years, why would he be nervous now?"

"Hush," I said, elbowing Kyle in the ribs. "It's sweet. He loves your sister very much."

"He better," Kyle muttered as the music swelled. I smiled and squeezed his hand, so glad that they were having such a beautiful day for the wedding. The sun was just beginning to set, casting a soft orange glow that mingled with the soft candlelight that surrounded the backyard. I had watched from the window as the hired wedding help had worked all morning transforming the space into the romantic setting that it was now. It was simple and perfect, just like the love that this couple was about to make official. A small group of about fifty were standing as the bridal march started from the three-piece orchestra in the background, with Kyle and I right next to his parents. He looked too handsome for his own good in a gray pinstripe with a shirt and tie to match his eyes. I had chosen a blue dress of my own, a gauzy number that left one shoulder bare and hugged my curves. The look on Kyle's face when I emerged from the bathroom told me what his mind was already thinking.

Unfortunately, we would have no time for hanky-panky afterward. Our suitcases were already packed and our boarding passes printed out for the last flight out of North Carolina tonight. There was no reason to stay any longer once he saw off his sister on her honeymoon. It saddened me to know that it was almost over, that we would be returning to reality in a few hours.

Nicole and her dad walked down the petal covered aisle toward Reese, and I sighed at how beautiful she looked in her simple gown, how Reese wiped back a tear as she approached the altar. Kyle pulled me closer to him and I resisted the urge to lay my head on his shoulder, instead watching as their father placed Nicole's hand in her soon to be husband's. In the span of a few minutes, it was all over and Reese was kissing Nicole, while everyone else was wiping their eyes and clapping.

"Just beautiful," Julia was saying, clasping her hands together as they walked back down the aisle. "Not what I would have wanted, but it suited them."

I chose not to respond as Kyle tugged me out of the aisle and toward the massive tent that would house the reception. "Why do women always cry at weddings?"

"Because we hope ours is just as beautiful," I said softly as we walked hand-in-hand behind his parents.

"And that we will be so lucky to find someone that loves us the same."

"Have you found that someone, Jess?" Kyle asked softly as we neared the entrance.

"That's a silly question, Kyle. If I had, I would already be married." I laughed hollowly, though my heart knew I had found someone very special indeed. "So lucky for you, I am still free and clear to do your dastardly deeds."

Kyle grunted and pulled us out of the line, away from the crowd and in the shadow of the house. "I haven't properly thanked you for this weekend, for all of your help."

"Oh, I think you have thanked me over and over again," I laughed as he grabbed my hands with his. "I do believe it was at least three times last night."

Kyle flushed a deep red and I bit back a grin myself, loving to see him embarrassed for once. "Still," he continued, clearing his throat. "I couldn't think of anyone else that would have made this as easy as you had. I appreciate all that you have done, Jess."

"Well, you are welcome," I responded, tugging at his hands. "Come on, I know your mom has some good food in that tent."

"Wait," he said, pulling me back in front of him before letting go to reach into his coat pocket. "I got you something for putting up with me."

"But you are doubling my salary, remember?" I teased, my throat going dry as he pulled out a small box tied with a green bow. *Don't even think that way, there is no way possible that would be what I would want it to be,* I told myself as I eyed the box.

"Yeah, well, I am going to do that too," he said, handing me the box. "This is something extra. Go on, open it."

My hands trembling, I pulled the ribbon and opened the lid, gasping slightly as I laid my eyes on the most perfect round diamond pendant I had ever seen. Wow, didn't see that coming whatsoever. It was gorgeous, a perfect cut, not that I expected anything different with Kyle. Under any other circumstance, I would be jumping up and down about this gift from this man, but the timing was all wrong, the reason was all wrong. He didn't need to pay me for the sex we had and that was what it felt like. "I-I can't accept this," I stammered, closing the lid and pushing it toward him. "Really. Thanks for the gesture but it wouldn't be right."

"But I bought it for you," he said as I forced the box back into his hand. The hurt look on his face was like a dagger to my heart, but I forced a smile as I closed his fingers around the box. "Any woman would be happy to have that, I swear, but not in this situation. You don't owe me anything for, well, anything."

He was silent for a moment as he looked at the box and then at me, his eyes full of conflict. "Well, I can't make you take it," he finally said slowly, placing the box back into his coat pocket. "But I feel like I owe you something."

"Not a thing," I forced out, grabbing his arm. "Come on, let's go join the party while we can."

***

"Well, here we are."

I nodded and grabbed my suitcase before it could go around the baggage claim again, giving him a smile as he helped me get it over the edge. "Yep, at least it was a smooth flight." And it had been. We had left as soon as the newlyweds had, giving our goodbyes to his family and hopping on the plane right before takeoff. The ride had been in silence, with me feigning sleep just to avoid the awkward conversation we were now forced to have.

"Are you sure you don't want a ride?" he was asking as we walked toward the exit, where a luxury car sat idling in the loading zone. "There's a car waiting for us. I will drop you off wherever you want."

"No, no I am fine," I stated, stopping right in front of the car. "Besides, it's out of your way to take me home. I can get my own car."

"I don't mind," he insisted as the driver took his suitcase. "Really, Jess."

I shook my head and pulled my coat closer to my body, the heaviness of the goodbye weighing on my heart. "Well, thanks for the interesting weekend. I enjoyed meeting your family and seeing your hometown."

Kyle's jaw worked as he looked at me, his blue eyes unreadable as he reached out and pulled me toward him, enveloping me into his arms. I fought back the tears as he hugged me close, his scent imprinting itself in my brain. I didn't want to leave him, hell, I didn't want to be denying the last ride we were going to have together but my heart couldn't take the sadness that was settling in. No matter how long I dragged it out, the end result was still going to be the same. I would go home to an empty bed, to the feeling that something was missing in my life. I would piece my heart back together and he would move on.

His hand went into my hair and I sniffed back a tear, his familiar touch causing my throat to burn with emotion. "Ah, Jess," he said, his lips grazing my forehead. "Come home with me, just tonight. We can give ourselves one more day."

"I can't," I forced out, though parts of me were screaming out otherwise. Pushing out of his arms, I wiped at my eyes and gave him a smile, noting that his expression was unlike anything I had ever seen from him.

"I never meant for this goodbye to be so hard," he said, touching my wet cheek. "I never meant to make you cry."

"I've got to go," I said, stepping out of his touch. "See you on Monday."

He opened his mouth to say something else, but closed it, nodding as he went for the car door. "Have a safe trip home then."

Chapter 12

I cried all the way home. The cab driver must have thought me to be crazy the way he kept glancing in his mirror but I didn't care. I hurt all over, already missing his presence, his touch. I gave the driver an extra tip and a watery smile as he hastily handed me my suitcase, his eyes wide as he wasted no time climbing back into his car and driving away.

With a swipe of my eyes, I climbed the stairs to my apartment and opened the door, where a startled Gretchen met me just inside.

"Oh honey," she exclaimed, taking my suitcase and closing the door.

"I-I…" I forced out, collapsing on the couch.

"I told you," she said softly, taking a seat next to me. "I knew you would fall in love with him. I think you already were before you left anyway."

"I don't need a lecture," I forced out, wiping my eyes with the back of my hand. "Really."

"Sorry, I just don't know what to say," she muttered, reaching for her phone. "Chinese or pizza?"

"Chinese," I said, knowing that she knew the only way to comfort me. She nodded and pressed the speed dial while I flung myself back on the couch,

Kyle's scent still clinging to my coat. I knew it was going to be hard, but I hadn't expected it to feel like this.

"Did you tell him?" Gretchen asked as she hung up.

"Tell him what?" I asked, flinging an arm over my eyes.

"Tell him how you feel."

"Yeah, right. Are you serious?"

"Well, he might feel the same," she said slowly as I looked at her with a frown. "I mean, how's to know nowadays anyway? Maybe you tamed the playboy. It's obvious something went on between you two or he wouldn't have kept having sex with you. Men might like easy women to have fun with but they also like that warm fuzzy feeling no matter what they say."

"Yeah, well, I don't think he had those types of feelings," I muttered, pulling off my coat and flinging it into the corner to get rid of his smell. I mean, he had given no indication or had I not read between the lines? We were talking about a man who had yet to commit to anyone or anything except his job. Of course he wouldn't spell it out to me, but did I dare hope? Did I dare wish? "Shit, you might be right," I said to Gretchen, jumping off the couch and grabbing my coat.

"Where are you going?" she asked as I retrieved my purse off the counter.

"I'm going to find out," I said, my heart hammering in my chest.

"Well, Chinese if it doesn't work out!" she called as I flung open the door and went down the hall. If it didn't work out I was going to need lots of Chinese and alcohol.

***

It took all of fifteen minutes for me to arrive at Kyle's house, anticipation and nervousness welling up inside as I paid the driver and walked up to the steps. I was about to take a big gamble with my heart; the rest of my life might depend on whether he took me in or left me on the street to nurse my broken heart.

With a deep breath I knocked on the door, once then twice as I realized it was well past midnight and he probably was already in bed. What was I thinking? This wasn't the time to be confronting him about his feelings for me! It could easily wait until tomorrow or the next day or I could just walk away, none the wiser.

"Are you going to stand there all night or are you going to come in?"

Surprised, I looked up to find Kyle above me, casually leaning against the doorframe, bare-chested and grinning. "I-uh."

"Come on in, Jess."

I gulped and moved inside, taking in the familiar surroundings with a grimace.

He shut the door and grabbed my arm, spinning me around to collide with his bare chest. His lips pressed down on mine hungrily as he pushed us against the foyer wall.

"I. Knew. You. Would," he said between kisses, his lips greedily tracing the arch of my neck. "God, I missed you."

"No, wait," I started as he began to shred my coat. "I'm not here for that."

Kyle stopped his assault and pushed away from me, running a hand through his hair. "What are you here for then? Did you forget something?"

"I did," I said softly, pushing away from the wall. I could see the way he was already closing up to me, the shuttered look moving over his handsome features, and sighed, touching my fingers to his bare chest, right above his heart. "I forgot to tell you I love you."

He stilled and looked away, his jaw working, and I felt my heart break in that moment. I had made a mistake, one that couldn't be taken back. "I'm sorry, I will go now."

"No," he said, pulling on my arm as I turned toward the door. "No."

I looked up at him and nearly stopped breathing as he smiled at me, a heart-stopping smile that touched my very core. "God, Jess, I love you too. I should have told you earlier but you were so insistent on riding in your own damn car. I thought you needed space so I was going to wait until tomorrow."

"Y-you love me?" I squeaked out as he pulled me against him, his hands framing my face.

"Hell yes I do," he said, kissing my lips gently. "You are unlike any other woman I have ever encountered. I would be a fool to let you go now."

"Oh Kyle," I breathed, not believing that this could be real.

"I have something for you," he said, pulling back from me as I thought of all the naughty things I was going to do to this man tonight. He freaking loved me! Me of all people in this entire world. This was beyond a dream come true and if it was a dream, I was going to refuse to wake up.

"I don't care what it is, just come back," I told him.

"Oh no, you aren't going to deny me this," he grinned, moving upstairs. "Be right back, love."

I nearly melted into the floor as I threw off my coat and shoes, doing a little twirl in the foyer. This was craziness. I was in love with this awesome man and he actually loved me too! I couldn't believe it, not in a million years.

His footsteps sounded on the stairs and I looked up to find him still grinning at me, his eyes mirroring my own. "Listen, I know we haven't been together in this capacity for long," he said, coming to stand right before me. "But I think I fell in love with you the night you threw up in my bathroom. From then on, I have thought about you, dreamed about you, Jess." He brought his hand in front of us, where a little box sat on his palm, tied with a green ribbon. "And this is for you. I won't accept no this time."

Remembering the necklace, I bit back an inward smile and took the box, more than happy to accept it now. Now, everything was different between us.

Pulling on the ribbon, I opened the lid and promptly dropped the box, my hands going to my mouth in surprise. No way.

Kyle laughed as he scooped up the box, dropping to one knee as he held it back up toward me. "I bought this before we left for the wedding. I was playing on a hunch and hoping to God I was right. I love you, only you and am perfectly happy with a long engagement if you would like before we marry as long as you promise not to ever make me come back to this house alone. Marry me, Jess, and make me the happiest damn guy on the planet."

"Yes," I squealed, throwing myself at him. "Oh my God, yes!"

Laughing, we fell to the floor, me landing on top of him as I kissed every inch of his face. "I love you so much. I swear this has to be a dream."

"A dream come true," he said softly, searching my eyes with his. I gave him a long, shuddering kiss before moving off him so we could both sit on the foyer floor, my hands shaking as he plucked the diamond ring out of the box and slid it on my finger, the gem twinkling in the light.

"This is so unexpected," I said softly, my eyes tearing as he kissed my hand. "Well, I guess I must put my resignation in now." Could I still work at his office as his fiancée?

"I don't give a damn if you do or not," he said immediately, his eyes twinkling with laughter. "You are one of the best damn paralegals I've ever had. I just want to know, how soon can you move in?"

Epilogue

"Are you sure you want to do this? We can hold off another month."

I smiled as I smoothed down the collar of his shirt, touching his cheek with my hand. "Love, you have to face them eventually. It might as well be before the wedding."

Kyle clenched his jaw but said nothing as we stood on the steps, watching as the taxi appeared in the distance. It had been six glorious months since that night in the foyer and I couldn't be happier. The firm was flourishing and since we had settled into his house, he had worked normal hours, spending every night here with me. I was still working at the office with Gretchen and there were days I woke thinking I was living in a dream, but none of it had disappeared yet so I was clinging to this reality that was now my life.

It had taken lots of discussion but Kyle's parents were finally coming for a visit to our house, to talk about the wedding we were going to have in two months and to repair their relationship with their son. Kyle was nervous even now. I could feel the tension in his body as he wrapped his arms around me, his chin on my head. "You know, you could have a beer or two before they get here," I said softly.

"I'd rather have you again," he answered, his hand tweaking the underside of my breast.

"Kyle," I warned, turning in his arms. "We don't have that kind of time." I then gave him a smile and reached up, brushing my lips against his. "But I do need to tell you something."

"What is it, love?" he asked, his eyes on mine.

"You are going to be a father," I blurted out, my heart bursting with love for this man. I had been super shocked myself when the faint line on the test had appeared.

"I… what?" he said, stunned as he looked at me.

"In about say seven months or so," I smiled.

"We are going to be parents," he said, kissing me hard. "Are you sure?" I nodded and he gave me a tender kiss, his hand drifting between us to touch the very small swell that had already appeared.

"Hot damn, I'm going to be a father."

"Yes indeed," I answered, covering his hand with mine. "Perhaps that will break the ice with your parents."

What to read next?

If you liked this book, you will also like *Two Reasons to Be Single*. Another interesting book is *Investment in Love*.

Two Reasons to Be Single

Olivia Parker has a job doing what she loves, a wonderful family and plenty of friends, but no luck in the love department. Tired of worrying about it, she decides to swear off love completely and focus on all the good things in her life. Just as she makes her firm resolution, Jake Harper arrives in town and knocks her plans into a tailspin. As the excited single ladies of Morning Glory surround the extremely attractive newcomer, Olivia steers clear of the "casserole brigade," as she calls the women, and tries to keep her distance from Jake. Instead, a variety of situations throw them together and they get to know each other better. They both have reasons for not wanting to get involved in a relationship, but the chemistry between them ignites, even as they desperately attempt to keep it at bay. As things heat up between Olivia and Jake, there is an aura of mystery about him that leaves Olivia certain that he is hiding something. When Jake disappears for a few days without telling Olivia that he is going out of town, she hates the way it makes her feel, and it reminds her of why she was giving up on dating in the first place. As Olivia's feelings for Jake grow, so does the need to find out what exactly brought him to Morning Glory and what he's been hiding.

Investment in Love

Calvin Barnard is a hard-working New York stockbroker, focused entirely on his job. His life is simple until the day he gets a call from the lawyer of his late Great-Aunt Loretta. The great-aunt he barely knew has left him $10 million and a house in the tiny backwoods Oregon town of Carterville—but there's one condition. Before Calvin can get the money, he has three months to marry a girl from that same rural town. Suddenly, everything is complicated, as Calvin tries to figure out how his reclusive great-aunt had millions of dollars, what he's going to do with her old dusty mansion, and which small-town girl will be willing to marry him on short notice. Interior designer Ellie Parker looks like the perfect solution to his problems: She's beautiful, single, and available to fix up the old house. But when Calvin starts to feel more than sympathy for sweet Ellie, he'll have to decide between the inheritance of a lifetime or the love of the most enchanting woman he's ever met.

About Emily Walters

Emily Walters lives in California with her beloved husband, three daughters, and two dogs. She began writing after high school, but it took her ten long years of writing for newspapers and magazines until she realized that fiction is her real passion. Emily likes to create a mental movie in her reader's mind about charismatic characters, their passionate relationships and interesting adventures. When she isn't writing romantic stories, she can be found reading a fiction book, jogging, or traveling with her family. She loves Starbucks, Matt Damon and Argentinian tango.

One Last Thing...

If you believe that *The Weekend Girlfriend* is worth sharing, would you spend a minute to let your friends know about it?

If this book lets them have a great time, they will be enormously grateful to you — as will I.

Emily

www.EmilyWaltersBooks.com